The Hollow–Eyed

Angel

The Hollow–Eyed

Angel

Janwillem van de Wetering

SOHO

Copyright © 1996 by Janwillem van de Wetering
All rights reserved.

Published by
Soho Press Inc.
853 Broadway
New York, NY 10003

Library of Congress Cataloging-in-Publication Data

Van de Wetering, Janwillem, 1931–
The hollow-eyed angel / Janwillem van de Wetering.
        p.   cm.
ISBN 1-56947-091-X
1. DeGier, Rinus (Fictitious character)—Fiction.   2. Grijpstra,
Henk (Fictitious character)—Fiction.   3. Police—Netherlands—
Amsterdam—Fiction.   4. Dutch—New York (N.Y.)—Fiction.
PS3572.A4292H65   1996
813'.54—dc20   95-26296
                                                            CIP

Book Design by Cheryl L. Cipriani

Manufactured in the United States of America

10 9 8 7 6 5 4 3 2

to Ed Burns (the father)

Chapter 1

"Yes," the gentleman whose name the commissaris hadn't quite caught said, "it's about my uncle, who is dead, murdered. And about my serving with the Police Reserve, for quite a few years now, serving the queen, and serving you too in a way. And that a thing like that can happen, in New York, that's terrible, don't you think so, sir?"

The commissaris, chief of detectives, municipal police, Amsterdam, Holland's capital, sighed. Because the gentleman (whose name—he said it again—was Johan Termeer) had added a question mark to his summing-up, an answer would be expected.

The commissaris could just say yes, that it was indeed terrible. That the world is not getting any better. That an uncle goes out for a quiet walk, in Central Park of all places, in New York, richest city in the most powerful country—God help us!—Sunday morning—the sun is shining—kids at play—music—balloons—and, inexplicably, the dear old man *dies* between the azalea bushes? That's terrible, yessir.

Not a witness anywhere to tell what caused his death. And, when his remains are finally found the next day, the entire lower part of uncle's torso has been consumed by beasts or birds or something. The dead body of your Uncle Bert, your only relative on earth, turns up in a goddamn *park*. Discarded. Robbed. Dismembered. Two loose legs and only the top part of the rest. The loved one's final breath rattled while, on the nearby freshly mown lawn, the Park Stompers struck up their next tune. Complainant Johan Termeer whistled, not unmusically, "When the Saints Go Marching In."

The commissaris frowned. "And the police?"

"The New York Police Department?" complainant asked. Well, the NYPD ignored the matter. They filed away the whole thing—the murder or manslaughter— under "heart attack," if you please.

"Now," complainant said, "if you are police yourself—okay, a Reserve, an unpaid volunteer, auxiliary, even so, that's some sort of cop, right?—does it help? Especially if you are in a faraway country?"

It had taken some time before complainant even learned that Uncle Bert was dead. Complainant heard it later, early the next day. Because of the time difference of six hours. It took a while before it occurred to Charlie, his uncle's neighbor, that he might inform the dead man's only relative that Bert Termeer was no longer with us. Okay, so that relative lived across an ocean but, jeez, what with modern phone connections, satellites and answering machines and so forth, it's no big deal to cross an ocean by voice. "Is it?"

The commissaris put in another frown, indicating that people's proverbial thoughtlessness is, indeed, despicable.

So what do you do? complainant continued.

You hand over your elegant hair-care establishment in Amsterdam's luxury suburb Outfield to partner Peter.

You yourself travel to New York, by the next Royal Dutch Airlines flight. You find the Central Park Precinct and you talk to the desk-sergeant. Okay. You *try* to talk. Your English could be better.

Does anything happen?

Nothing happens.

You're told this was an accident. Uncle Bert, out for a stroll in Central Park, got hit by a falling branch or something, or a ball, or a rock, right smack in his chest. This didn't kill him, but the heart attack did. Shock or something. That's Mr. Park Cop's verdict.

Jeez!

So what comes next? Flying home comes next.

And in the 707 you begin to think.

You are — right? — yourself Mr. Cop. And America—right?—and Holland, the Netherlands, are friendly countries. Aren't there all kinds of police connections between the two, re drug trafficking and bank fraud and whatnot? So why can't you get some justice going if you now think of the highest office you can reach—reach-ability, that's a factor—and you go and actually see that powerful godlike figure?

Who to use as go-between? How about Adjutant* Grijpstra? Grijpstra is a professional cop, a good guy, he taught you for a year at Police Reserve Evening School where you got your official police diploma.

And so, through the good offices of "Master Steel-brush," as Murder Brigade Detective Grijpstra is known, because of his silver-gray cropped hair, you do manage to enter the antique-looking command post of Amsterdam's chief-detective, and there sits "Mr. Little Old Gentle-man," as the commissaris is affectionately referred to within the force, and you are requested to state your case.

So you do that.

"Yes," the commissaris said, trying to enjoy the rare sunlight (Holland being an overcast country) that made the Oriental carpet between him and Johan Termeer glow mysteriously, especially where the orange designs almost touched the carpet's red border. He would have preferred the protection of his sculptured desk, which he had

* The ranks of the Amsterdam Police are constable, constable-first-class, sergeant, adjutant, inspector, chief-inspector, commissaris and chief-constable.

forfeited, because of the supplicant's being a policeman, not a bothersome civilian. The situation, between colleagues so to speak—he agreed with that—required an immediate face-to-face interview. The commissaris's and his visitor's identical leather-upholstered chairs were only separated by an old Chinese table, made from ironwood, a fine colonial piece from the former Dutch East Indies, on loan from the Netherlands Office of State-Owned Art.

The commissaris offered Verkade Assortie cookies from a tin, poured Egberts Gold Label coffee from a silver pot. This was Class A treatment. The visitor should take note.

Be easily approachable, even to lower rank and file, the commissaris instructed himself. An executive officer behaves "like a good father of the family."

In fact, he told himself, he had no time for all this nonsense. He had to go home, to his nice Queens Avenue residence where his wife, Katrien, would have lunch ready, to be served in the back garden: an open-faced beef sandwich, perhaps, a bowl of broth. At his advanced age chicken broth seemed to restore his frail body. He never used to go home for lunch but approaching retirement had weakened his discipline. A few more weeks and he was all done.

Chief-detective, personally in charge of Serious Crime. Renowned master of the famous Murder Brigade. Nice sounds, little substance. A drab little gent in a suit from yesteryear, bought in another epoch, in an expensive

Baerle Street Store, where salesmen bowed, might even scrape.

Did anyone still know what bowing and scraping meant?

You had to make your own selection from the racks these days and hearty salesmen slapped your shoulders, even tweaked your buttocks if you gave them half a chance.

"Commissaris?"

He looked up. "Yes, dear boy?"

"Could I have your comments?"

After Reserve Constable Termeer had said he wanted to be addressed as "Jo," the commissaris restated the complaint. "In Central Park, your uncle, Bert Termeer, was found dead last Sunday. Your uncle's neighbor Charlie telephoned to say that something bad had happened. Hearing that your uncle had died of an alleged heart attack in the park, you considered the situation suspicious and took the first plane to Kennedy Airport...."

The commissaris nodded helpfully, his inviting smile showing long yellow mousy teeth. "Is that correct?"

"That's correct, sir."

"Your English was good enough to enable you to understand Charlie's message?"

"Sumzing bat, Unkel det," Jo Termeer said in his best Amsterdam accent. "I watch lots of movies. *Det* means 'It's all over.'"

"Right," the commissaris said. "So neighbor Charlie knew your telephone number?"

"He found it in Uncle's desk," Jo Termeer said, remembering he was a policeman now, that he had to be precise. "Uncle Bert rented both his work and living space; Charlie was his landlord as well as his neighbor. Charlie had Uncle's keys. There were only the two of them in the whole big building. They needed each other. Uncle ran a mail-order business and Charlie sometimes helped him. Uncle Bert sold books. The building is on Watts Street, Tribeca, New York City."

"They weren't roommates?"

Termeer shook his head. "Charlie lives on the top floor. Uncle had the rest of the building. Separate households."

The commissaris switched tactics. He wanted to get to know complainant. "You flew out straightaway. Expensive?"

The ticket was cheap enough, Jo said, even at short notice. It pays to have friends.

"Friends?"

Termeer meant Marilijn, from the travel agency. Whoever was in with Marilijn traveled practically for free. He and Peter knew her.

"A personal friend?"

"Business. My partner, Peter, gives her free haircuts."

Marilijn threw in a New York hotel room too, with a view of an airshaft, but hey, sixty dollars.

"One moment," the commissaris said. His tape recorder's red eye no longer gleamed between milk jug and sugar bowl. He changed the battery. "Continue, dear boy. What did you do on arrival?"

"Found the police precinct that dealt with the incident, right there in the park, sir. I made inquiries, first of the desk-sergeant, then of a detective-sergeant, a man called Hurrell. Hurrell knew all about the case but wasn't sharing his information." Jo growled. "Goddamn asshole."

He was taken aback by his own profanity.

"I beg your pardon, sir."

Termeer blushed as he looked straight ahead, over the commissaris's shoulder.

Jo's features were flawless, the commissaris thought. Termeer would do well as an actor in commercials. A hero. The driver who stops for an old lady at a crossing. He who returns lost valuables. The magazine mannequin who brushes his teeth with the latest fresh-tasting soda and salt toothpaste.

Straight nose, firm mouth, nicely rounded chin, the commissaris thought grimly. The large sea blue eyes would be clearer if Termeer wasn't suffering, or, perhaps, frustrated. There might be some shyness here too, because he was a mere reserve constable who had penetrated police headquarters' superspheres. There might also be regret, after the use of bad language just now.

"You will inherit everything?" the commissaris asked pleasantly.

Termeer shrugged. "I'm the only relative but I'm not in need of money. Me and Peter own the hair-care. The shop generates piles of cash."

"Tax free?"

Termeer winked. "Right, sir. Me and Peter used to be socialists until we saw that we were supporting the silly people."

"You refer to the unemployed?"

"You know the big sign on the East Highway Homeless Shelter?" Termeer asked, worried that the commissaris might misunderstand. "Ever see that sign on your way home, sir? After working all day?"

The commissaris knew the sign well. It had been made and put up by the shelter's inmates.

"HEY SUCKERS!" the sign shouted. "DID YOU HAVE A NICE DAY ON THE JOB?"

Sixty percent of the Amsterdam population collected national assistance.

"You're no socialist, are you, sir?" Termeer was asking.

The commissaris reminded himself that he was in charge. Not to be distracted. One dead uncle. Was he dealing with a serious complaint here?

"What party do you vote for, Jo?"

"I don't vote, sir."

"Gave up hope?"

Since Year Zero. Jo explained the term. The year he realized that ever-multiplying humanity would strip the planet's surface was when he started rethinking his attitudes. He had come to see that "this will not get any better," that "hope leads to disappointment." Jo explained that he hadn't come to Year Zero on his own; he had to thank his partner. Peter was the wise one. Nature people were, by nature, wise. Peter, back in the former Dutch South American colony of Surinam, had seen the rain forest being cut down. It had to be cut down to feed the desire of a relentlessly growing world population.

"Give up all hope," nature person Peter would say wisely. "Enjoy what is still left. Practice detachment!"

The commissaris smiled.

Jo Termeer looked hurt. "You don't agree, sir?"

"Dear boy," the commissaris said, "what's so detached about demanding justice? Aren't you here to avenge your uncle's murder?"

His uncle was a free soaring spirit brought down by self-serving desire. Jo tried to formulate that insight. How the detached should defend the detached. Make an exception. Idealism, pure and clear. "The last hurrah, sir."

"More nature people wisdom? You're quoting your partner, Peter?"

When two men live together the spark of illumination could jump across. "Wouldn't you say so, sir?"

The commissaris thought about being illuminated by sparks coming from Katrien or Turtle. He nodded. "You and Peter live together?"

"Above the shop, sir. In Outfield, in a large apartment. The mortgage is paid off."

"Gay?"

"Yessir," Termeer said clearly.

"Quite," the commissaris said. Being gay was hardly a delicate matter these days, even in his own generation, now mostly out of commission, due to advanced age. Consenting adults, of course. Even so, the police are reactionary. Outmoded rules tend to be maintained. Within the police the Reserve was most old-fashioned. Volunteers were screened. Gay candidates, if they made a point of mentioning their preference, would not be admitted, not because of their homosexuality but for some other reason. The committee was manned by older dignitaries, retired staff officers, of the same useless type he—the commissaris looked grim—would soon belong to: conservative, senile....

He mumbled. "Old fogeys."

"Beg pardon, sir?" Termeer asked.

Nothing, the commissaris was just thinking. A Police Reserve screening would mean coffee, offering of cigarettes, a word of welcome. Candidates enter one by one. The chief fogey asks why the volunteer feels he has to "serve and protect" on his own time, without pay.

Any fascist inclination?

A power problem? A need to arrest prostitutes and feel them up in the cop car?

No?

Well, that's just fine then.

"Fellow committee members—I, as chairman, propose that this fine fellow be allowed to study at police school, evenings only, as he has a job to do during the day.

"I say let's have him learn how to fire a handgun. Let's put him in uniform. Let him pass all the required exams.

"He may wear the police shield pinned to his chest if he passes all hurdles. He will help guard the Olympic soccer games, prevent racists from throwing bananas at nonwhite opposition players, forestall Neo-Nazis from making hissing sounds to imitate gas faucets when Jewish players score. At Christmas time he can take care that no youngsters are trampled when St. Nick rides into the city.

"Haha. Right you are, son, you can go, you have been accepted. You're a Patriot. With the big P of pooplah. We thank you for wanting to serve the state. Please tell the next peon to step right up, will you?"

The commissaris didn't imagine that the Reserve Screening Committee would pass effeminate types, with earrings or embroidered waistcoats, but this Johan Termeer showed none of those symptoms.

The commissaris himself did not particularly dislike gay people. He did not particularly like them either. "Just like liking goldfish," he had said once, during happy hour. He had wanted to impress some high-ranking colleagues. Katrien wasn't impressed. Katrien thought her spouse was being stupid again. Rightly so. The commissaris nodded.

"Right, eh, Termeer. So, this Peter who you mentioned just now. You live together. For some time, I presume?"

"Twelve years." Termeer straightened his back proudly.

The commissaris observed that complainant also, apart from being handsome, looked neat. He quickly noted Jo's bleached linen pants, tan tweed sports coat, cream cotton shirt, silk necktie with a batik design. His boots were suede, recently steelbrushed to straighten the little hairs.

"Will there be a considerable inheritance?" the commissaris asked. "Uncle Bert owned a mail-order business?"

Termeer shrugged his right shoulder disdainfully. "Money, but who needs it? I'm doing okay."

"Tell me about your uncle's business."

"He sold books," Termeer said. "Via a catalogue. Spiritual books mostly. Used. He bought the product in secondhand stores, catalogued it in his mail-order publication and sent it out widely."

"A good business?" the commissaris asked.

Termeer held his head to the side. "A sizable list, and he sold at about three times cost, but he also had expenses." Termeer's head dipped. "Bad debts maybe. Dud checks."

The commissaris thought of his dead brother, Therus. Therus operated a mail-order business once, distributing a catalogue of automotive products and gadgets. A profitable line. Brother Therus died in his early sixties, in gridlocked traffic near the fashionable suburb of Laren, hooting and hollering, in his new silver-gray Mercedes Sport, behind a shaking fist. Therus had spent his profits on Swiss mountaintops, with young escorts.

"Your uncle was profit-motivated?"

Jo Termeer didn't think so.

"Uncle Bert was childless?"

"Never married," said Termeer.

"Gay?"

"Uncle used to be friendly with his landlady, Carolien, when he lived in Amsterdam."

"And he rented space in a New York building?"

"On Watts Street," Termeer said. "That's in Tribeca, in Manhattan, near the river. Used to be a warehouse, where women filled jars with Russian caviar. Charlie lived on top, Uncle had the basement and the first two stories. Huge spaces, huge. The basement is where the books are kept."

Charlie, Jo said, sometimes helped out in the book business, updating the computer, packing up orders. The Watts Street building looked dilapidated on the outside and the elevators resembled the big predator's cages in the zoo, but inside, in the living and work areas, everything was kept up nicely.

"You visited your uncle in New York City?"

"I went on a tour once," Termeer said. "A supervised outing, like the Japanese here in Amsterdam: guide up front, guide in the back and everybody waves colored plastic tulips. Hard to get lost that way. We saw bridges and museums. There was a day off and I called on Uncle Bert. And just now I went again, because he was dead." Termeer nodded and sighed. He said the word in his own English. "Det."

The commissaris flicked the lid off the Verkade assorted cookie tin. The tin had been rifled by Grijpstra and his assistant, Detective-Sergeant de Gier. The mocha-glazed biscuits and sugared ladyfingers, his favorites, were gone.

He offered the tin. "A nonpareil?"

Termeer thanked him and took the offered cookie.

"Grijpstra arranged this meeting," the commissaris said. "Do you know the adjutant well?"

"Everybody in the Reserve knows the adjutant well," Termeer said. "Master Steelbrush taught me at police school. How to write reports. What crimes are arrestable. He's a good teacher, funny but firm, won't accept slackness. And idealistic." Termeer looked serious, possibly moved. "He taught us to respect the civilians as well as how to serve the suckers."

"You're quoting Grijpstra?"

"The civilian suckers tend to get themselves in trouble," Termeer said in a fair imitation of the adjutant's gruff voice. "They hire us to get themselves out of that trouble."

Yes, the commissaris thought. What about Grijpstra

himself? Father of too many children, now mostly on welfare. Husband of estranged wife. Presently engaged to a former prostitute with considerable ambition.

The commissaris coughed. To business. This Termeer seemed to be a decent fellow, responsible, not without a sense of humor.

Appearances are deceptive.

Time to inquire into his background.

Be a little more familiar now. "Tell me, dear boy..."

Replying to the commissaris's questions complainant claimed to have been born in Squire-Hugo-Town, deep in the provinces. Son of small farmers, but not for long, for Jo's mother had left on the rear of a powerful motorcycle, a new BMW 1000 cc Twin, driven by a German she'd met during the World War II occupation. Jo's tone of voice implied, the commissaris felt, three serious charges. First, adultery, for Jo's parents were married during the war. The German being the enemy added treason. Jo, born well after war's end, couldn't be the German's son, but his mother's leaving constituted the abandonment of a small child.

Whoring and national-interest-betraying mother abandoned child to the care of an overworked husband. Jo's father went bankrupt. Then he hung himself in his barn, above his tubercular cows.

A country tragedy with not too bad an ending for the blond orphan...

("Your age at the time, Jo?")

("Eight, commissaris.")

...who was adopted by Uncle Bert in Amsterdam. Uncle Bert was then a street vendor at the book market at Old Man's Gate in the inner city. Uncle took good care of nephew, who graduated from high school and became a hairdresser. Then, when Jo was doing well, uncle emigrated to the USA.

"Any particular reason?"

Jo shrugged. Uncle was restless. Holland is a small country. He had specialized in English-language books on spiritual subjects. The American mail-order market was huge. He had always been American-oriented. There had been maps of America on the walls of the Amsterdam apartment. Uncle had done some traveling in America and had lived in Bangor, Maine, and in Boston. He preferred New York, where he had been living for some five years now, maybe.

"Quite a leap from the Old Man's Gate," the commissaris said.

"Yes, commissaris, an adventurous man, my uncle."

"Did Carolien join him?"

"She didn't want to," Termeer said. "She was ten years older than Uncle. Carolien looked young for her age and Uncle Bert old, but the difference was increasing. Besides, she had become ill."

"Is she still alive?"

Termeer shook his head. "It was MS, multiple sclerosis. She was becoming paralyzed. Her eyesight was

going. I called on her at times, in a home at the Leyden
Canal."

"A pitiful situation?"

"Not at all." Termeer seemed more relaxed now,
talking easily. When Jo was still a little kid, Aunt Carolien
would come to fetch Uncle, tease him on the stairs with
her French lace underwear and high boots. She would
wear a hat decorated with bird of paradise feathers. A most
unusual woman.

"Not a, eh …?"

"For money?" Termeer asked. He didn't think so.
He had seen Aunt Carolien with the milkman, and under
a mailman who was pulling back before pushing in, but
those were surely chance couplings, engaged in for sport.
Aunt Carolien owned the tall gable house and lived on her
rents. She also had investments.

"The home where she stayed while crippled was paid
for by Uncle?"

No, there was no need. She was a self-supporting
woman, self-ended too, without the now so acceptable
euthanasia agreement with the city doctors: comfortably
in her bath, after several double and cold jenevers, a plastic
bag tucked over her head.

Jo Termeer smiled.

The commissaris waited.

"Aunt Carolien," Termeer said. "I really liked her."

Termeer told the commissaris that the two, uncle and
landlady, would travel together. He was taken along a few

times. Once the three of them were in Paris, in a flea market, searching for old books. Uncle Bert saw an antique wheelchair but the merchant was an arrogant fellow, like so many Frenchmen, unwilling to deal with foreigners who maltreated his language. Later that afternoon they passed the wheelchair again. Carolien said, "I will be needing that soon." A premonition. The street merchant wasn't paying attention. Off went Aunt Carolien in the wheelchair, sagging to one side, drooling, spastic, her cheeks trembling, Uncle pushing the bizarre contraption, which was beautifully upholstered with fancy art needlework. One two three, gone!

"You too?"

Termeer grinned. "My job was to distract the merchant, pretend I was shoplifting, get myself caught and patted down. But there was nothing on me."

The commissaris nodded as he visualized the scene.

Termeer laughed. "I'll never forget it."

The commissaris inserted a new tape into his recorder while, hand raised, he mimed a request for silence.

"Right. What would be your age now?"

Jo Termeer had just turned forty.

A forty-year-old young fellow, the commissaris thought. Crewcut, well dressed, athletic, well mannered, well spoken.

"How long has Uncle lived in America?"

Uncle Bert had spent over twenty years abroad and Aunt Carolien had died four years ago.

The commissaris switched off the recorder. He promised to make inquiries, via Interpol and other more direct connections.

"You won't be going to New York yourself?" Termeer asked.

The commissaris excused himself. He was sorry but New York, surely his colleague would understand, was outside the jurisdiction of the Amsterdam Municipal Police. Besides, he was about to be retired.

"But…"

No, the commissaris was certainly not going to America. It wasn't that he didn't want to assist a colleague. The commissaris would see what he could do for the voluntary Reserve Constable-First-Class Johan Termeer, but he was not to indulge in exaggerated expectations.

The commissaris, thinking that his performance had been impeccable, now intended to go and sit behind his imposing desk, each leg of which was sculptured in the image of a growling seated lion. He got up with some effort, dragging his painful leg.

Termeer got up opposite the commissaris and kept getting up. Termeer, standing, was at least a foot taller than his superior, and looked down on him from that height.

A formidable opponent, the commissaris thought, peering up anxiously and to the sides, for Termeer had very wide shoulders indeed. Amazing that he hadn't noticed before how formidable his visitor was.

A matter of attitude? Superior and inferior had faced each other just like this, dwarf versus giant, after Termeer had been marched in by Adjutant Grijpstra, but then the commissaris was convinced of his own value: a staff officer in an imposingly furnished room. Did a perception of discrepancy in height increase with an intensification of feelings of guilt?

Termeer was still talking, in a more pronounced bass voice, which was not at all servile. "Yes, sorry I bothered you, right? Commissaris, I must have been thinking that all my years of free labor for the police department warranted, perhaps..."

The commissaris heard himself apologizing again.

Termeer bent over him. "You do visit the States sometimes, don't you? Adjutant Grijpstra said so. That you used to have a sister living there, and friends and so forth. That you were connected."

The commissaris's secretary, Antoinette, came in to gather cups and plates and "took the liberty" (in her own words, as it turned out that she personally knew complainant) "of interfering a little."

"You don't mind, do you, sir?"

The commissaris looked about distractedly, hoping this would be over soon. He tried to admire the still-glowing carpet, the portraits of chief-constables of long ago, the flaming geranium blossoms on his wide window-sills.

Her husband, Karel, Antoinette said, had helped to

JANWILLEM VAN DE WETERING

refurbish Jo and Peter's hair-care salon in Outfield.

A coincidence.

"You're with the Reserve, aren't you?" Antoinette asked Jo Termeer. She looked at the commissaris. "Another part-time cop serving the community without pay." She turned to Termeer again, with the intimacy caused by bonding while you are helping friends to lay a wall-to-wall carpet in an elegant place of business.

"Didn't you help to arrest that Yugoslav fellow?" Antoinette asked Termeer. "That wild man who shot a regular cop in the drug bust at Warmoes Street?"

"Small world," the commissaris said.

"That cop never healed properly," Antoinette said. "His right arm hangs down, but without Jo Termeer here he would be dead."

Jo told Antoinette that his uncle had been murdered in Central Park, New York. Quite some distance. Hard to reach, especially when your English is not good. Quite a problem.

"Got mugged?" Antoinette asked.

Jo gave her the highlights.

"The poor old man," Antoinette said. "And you're looking into this, sir?"

The commissaris didn't think so.

"There is an invitation in the mail, sir." Antoinette held up a large manila envelope. "A police congress in New York." Antoinette flicked specks of dust off the commissaris's right sleeve. "Beautiful out there, you know. Karel and I went last year. We saw all the Warhols and the aircraft carrier parked on the river. Karel says it is a work of art in a way. That horror and violence are art, too." Antoinette unfolded a leaflet that she had pulled from the envelope. "Your congress is about horror too, about violence today. Will you just look at this cover photo? A dead girl with spittle on her lips?" Antoinette closed her eyes. "Yech."

She opened them again, to smile at Termeer.

"Isn't he lucky, hey? That chief of mine. A free week in New York, and I get my taxes deducted from my paycheck. The High and the Mighty."

The commissaris looked surprised.

Antoinette beamed. Now that the commissaris was going to retire anyway and she was going to miss him dearly, the distance between them had lessened. She pushed a little against him and looked down on his balding head. "New York. Some city. And the mugging isn't so bad if you keep alert. Everything is so cheap there, and the food is different everywhere, and *everything* is different, and all those other kinds of people." Antoinette's eyes grew bigger. "And those *buildings*, all that glass!"

All parties were quiet.

"So, if you were going anyway," Termeer said.

The commissaris frowned. "I weren't."

Chapter 2

"He were," Detective-Sergeant de Gier said two days later. De Gier had Detective-Adjutant Grijpstra to tea at his apartment because Grijpstra had walked out on his girlfriend that evening.

"Oh yes, oh yes, oh YES?" Grijpstra had asked, stomping down the stairs at Nellie's.

Nellie kept a hotel at the Straight Tree Ditch. A water pipe had broken that day and food had burned. Reciprocal irritation prevented sexual togetherness from reaching the level of love.

"But it did," Grijpstra said.

"Maybe for you," Nellie said and tried to explain the idea "together" but Grijpstra heard only criticism.

He was tired, after several hours of questioning a junkie charged with breaking and entering. The junkie

[*24*]

kept falling asleep and couldn't quite remember where he had worked, the nature of the loot and where or to whom he had sold it.

"Or maybe not," the junkie said after every statement, not so much because he wanted to obstruct the course of justice but because he wanted, philosophically, to indicate relativity and the chaotic nature of All and Everything.

"But what do you know?" the junkie asked Grijpstra. "Eh? You loutish moron. You should try the drug yourself, man, then you'll be on God's steps. Won't have to try to figure out what's what anymore. Won't bother free souls like me."

Grijpstra extracted croquettes from a vending machine in Leyden Street. He could have gone to his own place, a neat upstairs apartment on the Linenmakers Canal vacated some years ago by his family. He had, in order not to be reminded of her, urged his wife to take most of the furnishings. He had never redone the large rooms. The idea at the time was that "an intelligent man really needs little." Now it often seemed as if the empty space had no need of Grijpstra. "Pure emptiness illuminated by the glow of the void," chanted poet Grijpstra when She and the Noisy Ones got the hell out. That day the sun was shining.

Appearances change. He now saw the empty apartment as an extension of Holland's overall overcast climate. "Drafty absence of necessities partly illuminated by a dangling bare bulb," composed poet Grijpstra.

A Turk listened in. The Turk was a dismal import, once welcomed by the Dutch to perform tedious hard labor. Automation made the Turk superfluous. He was on the dole now, for his residential permit was permanent. The Turk was a thin man in a threadbare coat waiting, like Grijpstra, for a streetcar to splash along. The Turk raised wispy eyebrows. "You speak, friend?"

"Inspired," Grijpstra said, "by that empty space I call home, I am composing a poem."

He repeated his line. "Drafty absence..."

The Turk smiled. "You subtle soul."

Grijpstra acknowledged the compliment by sneezing.

The Turk wished him gesundheit.

It rained harder. Grijpstra shuffled backward into the protection of the tramway shelter. The Turk imitated the big man's movements. Raindrops jumped back from the tarmac and lashed the two men against their ankles.

"Home," Grijpstra said, "empty, quiet."

The Turk knew the words but had forgotten their meaning. "Two wives," the Turk said, "two TVs. Five kids moving between loud screens forever. Upstairs neighbors fight on bare boards."

"You speak good Dutch," Grijpstra said.

"Not all that difficult," the Turk said peevishly. "Not too many words, no grammar to speak of."

Grijpstra liked that. He passed the Turk a croquette from his paper bag.

"Pig?" the Turk asked suspiciously.

"Calf," Grijpstra said generously.

The Turk said that he had been known to eat pig. Not by mistake either. The Turk was against religious rules that bully. The Turk would consume, Allah be praised, whatever he liked, but if he did eat pig it would be nice to be aware of his sinning. His eye caught the flash of a car's brake lights. The Turk swallowed, smiled, straightened his back, recited: "At alien streetcar stop in slashing darkness my soul glows sudden red, lit up by sin."

Grijpstra applauded a fellow artist.

The Turk said that he found it easier to compose poetry in Turkish but had learned to express himself within the local limitations. So far his Dutch poetry had been of a lower level. He raised a finger.

"Convincingly wags tail the alien mutt

after been kicked silly in the butt.

"Doggerel." The Turk nudged Grijpstra. "You like?"

Grijpstra nudged the Turk. "I like."

The calf-croquette-chewing Turk stepped into his streetcar. "Blessings, friend."

Grijpstra waved. "Blessings."

The adjutant took a bus to the suburb of Outfield. He could have telephoned first. He had, in fact, held the coin the public phone would require but returned the guilder to his waistcoat pocket. Say de Gier was not at home—then Grijpstra would not have to make the bus ride, but he liked sitting and staring in crowded buses, "sharing meaningless silence with perfect strangers."

De Gier was home but didn't open up because he was listening to recorded jungle music from Papua New Guinea.

Grijpstra banged on the door and kept his finger on the buzzer.

"Tabriz," de Gier told his cat, "they have returned. Mind if I shoot through the door?"

"Gestapo," Grijpstra shouted because de Gier had Jewish ancestry and often discussed revenge. "Just once, Henk," de Gier would say. "I would feel so much better. You wouldn't mind, would you?" De Gier's Jewish grandmother had been run over by a bus in Rio de Janeiro after fleeing Holland just before the German occupation. De Gier's desire to get even was, in principle, based on Good versus Evil. He considered himself to be good. Good guy kills bad guy. After, maybe, slapping him around some.

While waiting for this opportunity de Gier went out of his way to be helpful to German tourists. He was also known to be particularly thoughtful when dealing with German suspects.

Perhaps, he told Grijpstra, only the fantasy mattered.

"Gestapo, my dear." Grijpstra leaned against the creaking front door.

De Gier opened the door suddenly, hoping that his victim would tumble into the room. Grijpstra had stepped back, however.

"I prefer to be alone tonight," de Gier said, making way so that Grijpstra could enter. "I am sure you understand."

Grijpstra was glad to know someone who put the kettle on to boil water for tea and who dropped bread slices into a toaster. De Gier, ten years younger than the adjutant, looked *filmish*, Grijpstra thought. The sergeant's short curly hair had been washed and conditioned, his large full mustache was brushed up. He ambled gracefully about in a striped cotton kimono. Mister B movie, Grijpstra thought kindly: our Action Hero, momentarily at rest, between fighting and fucking.

"How is Whatshername doing?" Grijpstra asked when de Gier pushed tea, anchovy toast and napkins, tastefully arranged on a dented silver tray, across the table.

"I don't understand Whatshername," de Gier said.

"I do understand Nellie," Grijpstra said, feeding fish to de Gier's cat, Tabriz. "Nellie wants me to move in but her hotel is too noisy." He brushed crumbs off his pinstripe suit. "I still prefer Living Apart Together."

"I prefer Nothing At All," de Gier said.

Grijpstra had heard inactivity proclaimed as solution, mere hours ago, by the junkie-burglar. But the junkie allowed for exceptions. There was the needle of course. "There could also be," the junkie had suggested respectfully, "direct divine connection via pussy."

"You dare to do away with your sexual quest?" Grijpstra asked.

"Man may dream," de Gier said.

"Of liberty?"

"Yes, by means of doing nothing. Don't you believe in total negation?"

"I believe," Grijpstra said, "and he who believes is not sure and therefore condemned to keep trying."

Both detectives, in the continuing dialogues, brought up the commissaris as their ultimate authority. The commissaris kept trying to approach the mystery via activity, useful work.

Serving the common good.

Why else would the commissaris go to America now?

Grijpstra sang "When the Saints Go Marching In."

De Gier reached for his trumpet and played the phrase on his instrument. He put the trumpet back.

Grijpstra explained what he knew of the case so far.

"Jo Termeer mentioned that tune?" De Gier stretched his foot toward the cat who rolled over on her back expecting a massage. "How did Jo know the Saints were marching while Uncle Bert was dying? Jo wasn't there, he was here, cutting hair in this very suburb, in Outfield."

Tabriz meowed pleasurably, but loudly, while her master's toes kneaded her bare belly. De Gier kneeled next to the cat. He circled Tabriz's mouth with thumb and index finger, and tightened his grip rhythmically. Tabriz meowing became structured into a musical "wah-wah-wah."

"I spent most of the afternoon questioning Jo

Termeer," de Gier said. "If I am collaborating on this case I would like to be properly briefed. I wasn't told about the Saints. I could have caught Termeer in a contradiction."

He frowned at Grijpstra.

"Termeer's information is based on double hearsay," Grijpstra said. "Uncle Bert's neighbor, landlord and part-time help, Charlie, told Jo that the song was being played when Uncle Bert was seen last. Charlie was told by passersby who were there at the time. Charlie is no witness either."

"Did neighbor Charlie interview possible witnesses to Uncle's death?" de Gier asked.

"Musical saints supposedly marched," Grijpstra said. "Not only that, an elderly couple was seen—foreign tourists—pointing out an alleged corpse to a mounted policeman." Grijpstra shook his head. "A police*woman*, I should say."

"Aha aha," de Gier said, "all news to me, friend. So you kept the information hidden so as to hear from me what Jo would come up with when I questioned him."

"Jo Termeer didn't mention an elderly tourist couple? Middle class? Foreign?"

"No," de Gier said. "Young Termeer reported he called at the Central Park Precinct and saw the desk-sergeant. The cop only knew about a dead derelict, found under a filthy blanket, a homeless person dressed in rags, and told complainant that an investigation was in progress."

"Embarrassment of corpses?" Grijpstra asked. "America the violent? Dead bodies galore?"

"Same body," de Gier said. "Charlie had identified the corpse as his dead neighbor. Termeer also saw a Sergeant Hurrell at Central Park Precinct. There was the language barrier again. Hurrell may have said that he would keep Termeer informed."

"No sense," Grijpstra said sadly. "It never makes sense. It never will either, unless we attempt to put it there. Show me your flimsy construction of how the facts we have determined might possibly connect."

"I don't construct in my free time," de Gier said. "It should be your free time too. Why bother me? Bother Nellie. Paint dead ducks in your empty apartment. Go home and play your drums."

In order to placate de Gier, Grijpstra recited his newly found, improved, partly stolen and combined poetry.

"Pure emptiness illuminated by the void's divine glow,
or is it a cold absence of necessities
lit meaninglessly
by a dim bulb suspended from a peeling ceiling?
I flee either choice and wait, in wet slashing darkness,
at an alien bus stop,
where my soul glows red in sinful flashes."

De Gier made Tabriz do more "wah-wah-wah." After that he applauded.

"I wasn't going to the whores," Grijpstra said.

"You were coming to me," de Gier said. "To try and fill your void with meaningless work." He smiled forgivingly. "Okay. I will humor you."

While making his report de Gier used the singsong of his native Rotterdam dialect which never failed to make Grijpstra crack up. "Please," sobbed Grijpstra. "Cut it out. Can't you speak like real people?"

Tabriz got hiccups and had to be picked up, turned over and shaken gently.

Seriousness returned.

De Gier reported, using the proper Amsterdam dialect, that Reserve Constable-First-Class Jo Termeer, during the course of an in-depth interrogation ordered by the commissaris, had made a good impression.

"Define *good*," Grijpstra told de Gier.

De Gier explained that Termeer seemed modest, polite, reliable, concise in stating his complaint. Not a dumb fellow by any definition. Perhaps lacking in education. "Like yourself," de Gier said. "Talented, diligent, but not somebody who questions reality."

Grijpstra recognized the type. "No quest. Energy spent on artful hobbies. Termeer is into Sunday painting? Dabbles in music perhaps?"

De Gier found and consulted his notebook. "Critical viewing of movies."

"Ah," Grijpstra said. "What kind of movies?"

"Action and bizarre."

"What kind of action?" Grijpstra asked.

"Fighting movies."

"What kind of bizarre?"

"Don't know," de Gier said.

"You didn't pursue that query?"

De Gier shook his head. "Jo likes movies set in Australia."

"Bizarre Australian movies?"

De Gier nodded. "And futuristic."

"Bizarre Australian futuristic action movies," Grijpstra summarized.

"That's it," de Gier said.

"Sexual preference?"

"Movie?"

"Termeer," Grijpstra said.

"Right, homosexual, lives with a colleague called Peter."

"Did you meet with Peter?"

De Gier, after the interrogation of complainant Jo Termeer at police headquarters, had driven over to Outfield, picked up Peter at the hair-care salon and interviewed Jo's partner in a nearby café.

"Direction of interview?" Grijpstra asked.

"Straightforward," de Gier said. "I told Peter that we were analyzing a complaint and checking some background."

"Showed your police I.D.?"

"Sure. Of course."

"Describe subject."

De Gier described Peter as a slender, active, intelligent forty-year-old black male. Fashionably dressed.

"Overdressed?"

"No."

"Mannerisms?"

"Effeminate?" de Gier asked. "No."

"How black?"

"Midnight black."

"Made a good impression?" Grijpstra said. "Right? You liked Peter."

"Yes," de Gier said. "Sure."

"Believable?"

"That's right."

"You discussed your admiration for black jazz with Peter?"

"I did not," de Gier said.

"And friend Peter thinks that Termeer is right to consult the Amsterdam Murder Brigade re the possible criminal nature of his uncle's death?"

"Yes," de Gier said. "I really liked that Peter."

"Biased," Grijpstra said. "You are biased, Rinus. You like midnight-black-skinned men because they remind you of Miles Davis, who plays trumpet the way you want to play trumpet but can't."

De Gier shrugged.

Grijpstra looked critical. "Unacceptable associations. Preconceived ideas, the wrong way round. Peter could still be unreliable. You agree, don't you?"

"Cut it out," de Gier said. "The opposite isn't true either. Although I dislike most pink-skinned folks who don't play the trumpet the way I would like to but can't, I can still appreciate reliability in you."

Grijpstra blinked.

"Sentence too complicated?" de Gier asked.

"Okay," Grijpstra said. "Complainant's partner, Peter, checks out. So does Termeer." Grijpstra paused. "Workwise too?"

"As a hairdresser, you mean?"

"Please," Grijpstra said. "As a cop."

De Gier read his notes, made that afternoon at Warmoes Street Police Precinct, in Amsterdam's Red Light District. Termeer, as auxiliary, had served there for some years now, doing evening duty and also working weekends. Two Warmoes Street Precinct uniformed sergeants, interviewed separately, stated that Termeer would show up two or three times per week. Such zeal, they declared, was unusual for voluntary policemen, who aren't expected to put in that much time on active duty.

"Did you hear about his participation in the arrest of a Yugoslav gangster?" Grijpstra asked.

De Gier found the note. Firearms were used. Termeer jumped the suspect after a professional cop had been wounded and brought down. Suspect struggled free. Termeer ran Suspect down after a long chase along alleys and canal quays. The spectacular arrest earned the reserve constable-first-class a special mention for bravery beyond the call of duty.

"Outperformed the professionals, yes?" Grijpstra asked.

"Yes," de Gier said.

"Whatdoyouknow," Grijpstra said. "A disciple of mine, Rinus. It's me who guided this good man for years. By my example, experience, expertise..."

De Gier read on. On another occasion Termeer arrested an armed and violent whoremonger.

"Details?"

Seventy-year-old German suspected of abusing a prostitute. Suspect, flashing a handgun, resisted arrest but was disarmed by Termeer using judo.

"Gestapo Untergruppenfuehrer on weekend leave from a federal prison in Bonn, Germany, nostalgically reenacting World War II atrocity," Grijpstra said. "And you were home, watching a video of cannibals from New Guinea. Wasn't Herr Müller lucky? *You* would have pulled out his toenails."

"Yeah," de Gier said. "Hurting an old man with a personality problem." He scratched behind Tabriz's ears. "What was Termeer like as a police school student?"

"Good," Grijpstra said. "Passed the final exam summa cum laude."

"Any fawning? Bending over backwards?"

Grijpstra nodded. "Some. Sure."

"Tough guy syndrome? Bought special equipment and clothes in the police store? Nazi boots? Leather coat?

Expressed interest in arresting young sailor types on bicycles without proper rear lights?"

Grijpstra shook his head.

"Negative observations?"

Grijpstra recalled a neatly dressed soft-spoken student who paid attention, made neat notes, didn't ask silly questions, arrived on time, didn't miss lessons, drove a clean and undented Volkswagen Golf.

"Not a nutcase?" de Gier asked.

"No."

De Gier's head moved closer to Grijpstra's. "Why," de Gier asked, "would, if you please, a non-nutcase desire to voluntarily join the Amsterdam Police to serve without pay?" De Gier dropped his voice dramatically. "Henk, listen. Isn't that, in itself, suspicious behavior? What we policemen are dealing with is human filth, misery any decent being would want to stay away from. And this good guy *volunteers*?"

Grijpstra grinned. "You mean that the very idea of wanting to be a cop is despicable in essence?"

"You disagree?" de Gier asked.

"Ask complainant," Grijpstra said. "I'm not being investigated here, okay?"

"I did ask complainant."

"You got a clear answer?"

"Termeer said he liked our type of work."

The detectives had more tea. Tabriz was turned upside down and kneaded by Grijpstra this time. The cat purred dutifully.

"Why," de Gier asked, "did you join the police yourself?"

Grijpstra cited stupidity, ignorance of choices, a slavish desire to serve the ruling class, a sadistic inclination. Uniform, badge, the right to carry arms are ways to indulge power.

He stared into de Gier's eyes. "And you, my dear?"

De Gier said that he wanted to serve the queen and that one could see the queen, or her symbol, the crown, as a kind of opening, a tunnel through which the aware and diligent disciple could approach divinity, even here on earth.

"That's nice," Grijpstra said.

De Gier poured boiling water into his teapot. "So what else do we know?" de Gier asked. "The commissaris mentioned that Termeer, according to Antoinette, appeared to be a 'young fellow of forty.'"

"Some young fellow," Grijpstra said. "Six foot two, a sporting type, physically not unlike yourself but mentally more pure. Less cynical, I mean."

De Gier had the same impression. Termeer could be described as childlike. As "nice."

"You told that to the commissaris?" Grijpstra asked.

De Gier said he had but that, in spite of the possibly authentic complaint, now sustained by a profile drawn up by an experienced criminal investigator...

("Meaning you?"

"You too somewhat," de Gier said.)

…he didn't think it was fair that because of Grijpstra, via his pushy introduction of his star student, complainant Jo Termeer, the commissaris was now more or less forced to jump into a risky set of circumstances. In a dangerous city like New York of all places. Right before the rheumatic little old gentleman was to be retired.

Grijpstra felt bad.

Chapter 3

"Grijpstra should feel bad," Katrien said.

The commissaris was having breakfast—a Sunday morning ritual comprising a choice of three cheeses, fruit juices in antique tumblers, perking coffee, which set him up for the day.

Since Katrien no longer smoked she had done away with breakfast. Her sudden gain in weight distressed Katrien. The commissaris kept saying he liked her "lady-like figure."

"You like nothing better than being a hero in America," Katrien said, "another ruse that you hope will make your image live forever."

The commissaris, squeezing a fresh roll, spilled crumbs.

"Or would this case be somehow special?" Katrien

asked. "A nasty twisted puzzle requiring your exclusive genius perhaps?"

The commissaris butchered a new piece of Gruyère.

"What is so peculiar about an Amsterdam book dealer found dead in Central Park, New York?"

The commissaris got up, walked over to his cylinder desk and came back carrying a fax that he handed over.

Katrien read that the commissaris's colleague Hugh O'Neill (a high-ranking detective with the New York Police Department, the commissaris explained) was nominally in charge of investigating the case of Bert Termeer, deceased, this fourth of June, in Central Park. The dead body had been found dressed in rags and covered with a filthy blanket. The autopsy indicated a fatal heart condition aggravated by trauma, an injury caused to Termeer's chest. A fallen branch was found near the corpse. Termeer's case was about to be defined as death due to natural causes, or caused accidentally, without intent. A sport-related incident hadn't been ruled out.

"The book dealer was struck by an unidentified implement, possibly propelled or wielded by an unknown party?" Katrien asked. She had been to New York and tried to recall a visit to Manhattan's Central Park. "Don't people play ball there?"

"This case is about to be closed," the commissaris said. He sipped apple cider. "A piece of cake, Katrien. Mere routine. I'm only looking into it in order to help out a nephew of the deceased, a policeman known to

Grijpstra."

"Do book dealers wear rags in New York?" Katrien asked. "Do they sleep in parks under filthy blankets?"

The commissaris said he planned to look into those controversial aspects.

"Maybe golf," Katrien said. "Or baseball, or something. Victim was hit, collapsed, crawled into the bushes?"

The commissaris nodded.

Katrien was still thinking. "No. Wouldn't he be more likely to stay in the open, where help would be forthcoming?"

The commissaris fetched more fresh rolls from the kitchen.

"A busy park within the metropolis," Katrien said. "A man has a heart attack. Wouldn't people notice?"

The commissaris agreed.

"What age was Grijpstra's pal's dead uncle?" Katrien asked.

"Seventy, Katrien."

"Enjoying good health, apart from the heart condition?"

The commissaris said he would inquire.

"Not a drunk? Or an addict? So why would he wear rags?"

The commissaris planned to find out.

Katrien, frustrated, ate something after all—thinly sliced cheese—and drank coffee, no cream, no sugar.

The commissaris played with his roll, then handed

the rest to her.

"Looks like it is all over," Katrien was saying. "What do you expect to come up with, Jan? Old people don't respond well to shock. They tend to just keel over. Remember my father?"

"Uncle Bert wasn't married," the commissaris said.

Katrien interrupted her eating. "Meaning what, my sweet?"

The commissaris meant that when Katrien's father died, he hadn't just switched off. He had been gradually worn down by seventy years of irritation caused by life's vicissitudes. That he was also hit by a truck was because, exhausted, he was paying no attention.

Katrien stared at her husband.

"I don't mean that you irritate me," the commissaris said. "Don't worry, Katrien. I'm sure the case is simple, even if it seems puzzling when we look at it from here. I'll check the details, ask around a little bit, study the location, go into this Uncle Bert's background. I'm sure my final report will put complainant's mind at rest."

"You'll be mugged," Katrien said. "You've been very sickly lately. You hardly sleep at night. You don't even enjoy napping. You keep taking pain pills. And I can't go with you because of our daughter's due date. I won't let you go."

Soon, the commissaris said, he would be retired. All the rest a man could ask for. He would wallow in nondoing.

"I'll go with you," Katrien decided.

"You promised to be here for the grandchildren's birth."

There was that—twins were about to be born to Katrien and Jan's youngest daughter. The birth was predicted to entail some complications. Katrien had promised support.

"I'll be fine," the commissaris said.

Katrien wanted to do something. The police convention accommodations consisted of a room in a Holiday Inn. Katrien had inherited a small fortune in tax-free jewels from a tax-evading aunt who had left her the key and authorization to enter a Swiss bank's safety deposit box. Katrien never wore "trinkets." She had sold the stashed rubies.

"I'll get you a nice hotel room. Right on the park. That will be pleasant. Maybe that place near that enormous museum. The Cavendish? I'll get you a suite. You can rest and enjoy room service."

The commissaris didn't hear her.

"You are thinking of something," Katrien said.

His attitude didn't change.

"Stop stirring your coffee, dear." She took away his spoon.

He looked at her over the rim of his cup.

"You don't have a premonition, do you?" Katrien asked. "I have one myself. Or was it that dream you were going to finish telling me about this morning? About the driver of a Number Two streetcar? You did tell me something but I kept dozing off."

"The Angel of Death," the commissaris said. "The driver was an angel. The message had to do with death, but not mine, I don't think."

"Good," Katrien said. She worried—about his frail health, the strenuous journey he was about to undertake, his coming retirement.

He helped his wife wash up.

"Will you tell me about that dream now?"

The commissaris busied himself stacking plates in the cupboard.

"Don't put that funny look on," Katrien said. "I know that look. That streetcar driver was a woman, wasn't she now? I know the one you mean."

"Which one?" he asked.

"That blonde? Long legs in the glass driver's cabin, glass all the way down to the street. On the new type of streetcar. You forget we were together when you noticed that lady driver. You were all eyes. You wouldn't talk much afterward."

The commissaris admitted that the driver had made an impression, had set off an erotic fantasy. The new model Amsterdam electric streetcars had all glass fronts, enabling the drivers to see in every direction. The drivers were therefore visible themselves. A long-legged female driver on a Number Two streetcar had made an impression. The woman displayed her body well. She wore a miniskirt and had a magnificent hairdo. She sat there like a prostitute in a window in the inner city, proud of her qualities, pretending not to notice men leering, possibly drooling. As a tram driver in uniform she was unapproachable, of course—the tram's radio connected to all police cars. This unapproachable status made the fantasy even stronger. "But the dream wasn't really all that sexy, Katrien. I mean, nothing happened."

Katrien smiled sincerely. "Enjoy your naughty dreams, Jan."

"It was more like a mystical dream," he insisted. "There was an extra meaning. More like divine, Katrien." He looked up. "One doesn't have sex with angels."

"Yes, right," she said kindly.

He was arranging the silver, forks with forks, knives with knives, neatly lined up in their drawer.

"Jan," Katrien said sternly, "is that why you use public transport nowadays? You want to be near that long-legged blond driver again, have her take you where she wants to?" She patted his cheek. "And you have such a nice car."

"I don't use the Citroën anymore because there is no more parking in town, Katrien." He sighed. "Not unless one tolerates the exorbitant charges. Last time I tried I was delayed and they put a boot on one of my tires. Another enormous hassle. A fine. I had to stand around while they took the boot off."

"It's all right," she said kindly. "When was the last

time you saw that angel driver? In reality, I mean."

It was the day he had received the auxiliary policeman.

"They don't issue miniskirts to tram drivers," Katrien said. "That beauty you and I saw had the garment cut short herself."

"Yes, Katrien."

"Bah." She glared at him. "I used to have nice legs too, but you never noticed."

"I did, Katrien." He smiled. "They still are very nice."

"You're not going to be a dirty old man, are you?"

He said he didn't think so.

She laughed. "You look worried."

He thought he looked more frightened than worried. He had just remembered that the dream driver had no eyes.

"A hollow gaze, Katrien."

Katrien liked to understand dreams. She tried to analyze his. Did he feel encouraged by the seductive angel? Was she urging him to cross the Atlantic? Was there any connection between the mystical presence and his future retirement? Very often male retired high officials couldn't bear to lose their sense of importance, respect, their self-esteem. They withered away or met with accidents or took heroic risks while they still could. Like the commissaris, at the end of his career, reaching out into a region where he would have no protection.

He didn't know what to answer.

"You're really going on this wild goose chase, aren't you?" Katrien asked.

The commissaris nodded.

She shook her head. "You'll get bashed yourself. Parks in big cities aren't the safest of places. You'll be another corpse in the azalea bushes."

Later that day she waved a travel guide, borrowed from a neighbor, at him. "It says right here: Central Park should be avoided after dark. Even during daylight solitary hiking is not encouraged on paths that seem deserted." She banged the book on his desk. "Isn't that terrible? Guidebooks are supposed to promote travel and even so they warn you off."

He said he'd be all right.

She showed him a folder advertising the Cavendish Hotel. "Nouvelle cuisine, Jan, you might like that. Here, look at this spread." He admired the displays of mini-helpings on maxi-plates. The plates were surrounded by dishes filled with gleaming fruit, jars of shiny candied foodstuffs, flasks filled with glowing wines or juices. There were elaborate flower arrangements too. He also studied a photograph of a Cavendish suite: a complete apartment— air-conditioning, every luxury provided. "You can watch nice movies."

Australian movies, the commissaris thought. He had read de Gier's report, specifying what Jo Termeer liked. The commissaris didn't care for action movies himself but liked simple drama. He remembered an Aussie film featuring a drunken party. Each guest had to bring his own pornographic object. One guest brought an attractive woman, who set out to seduce the host. The party didn't end well. There were arguments and disappointments. Sunrise found the host watching his car being driven into a tree by guests.

She pointed out furniture to him: a four-poster bed, Chippendale couches. Yes, he would be able to lie down there.

"And a view of Central Park. You'll be looking down on all your suspects."

He looked at the rates. "But so much money, Katrien."

"Aunt Koba's present."

The inheritance, of course, he thought.

"And you won't stay long, will you?"

Not at those prices.

"Kiss me," she said.

They embraced.

Later that Sunday the commissaris walked in the rear garden of his house at Queens Avenue, between three-foot-tall weeds. His pet turtle, waiting for lettuce leaves, made swaying movements on his private rock.

"Let's hope we face no evil out there," the commissaris told Turtle. "Katrien is probably right. A showdown in Central Park could be bloody. Hooliganism, gang-related. And I would be alone. This Detective Hurrell doesn't appear very alert."

Turtle chewed more lettuce.

"Never mind?" the commissaris asked. "Jo Termeer insists that God is Good and Justice will be Achieved and who am I to argue with Positive Thinking?"

Turtle, sarcastically, closed one eye.

"I'm doing this because I am getting very feeble now?" the commissaris asked. "My last chance to win medals?"

Turtle started one of his slow dances.

"Katrien is right?" the commissaris asked. "Realizing I am entering my Final Agony now I plan a last fling? I will be all set to lose my life there spectacularly after setting things right?"

Turtle gummed more lettuce.

"I don't have any teeth either," the commissaris said, baring his long dentures, fair enough copies of what had once been real, craftily shaded a pale ivory hue. "Pure plastic, my dear."

Turtle swallowed, looked up expectantly.

"Or is this one of these instances that calls for detachment?" The commissaris winked. "We do this for Nothing? We don't walk the way that can be called a way? No, Turtle, we surrender." The commissaris smiled down on the reptile. "We are merely aware, we meditate, we gain ultimate insight."

Turtle heightened the rhythm of his dancing feet and

shaking shield.

"Too Zen for me perhaps," the commissaris said. "Even now, when my working life is almost over. Who am I fooling? Career does matter to me. I'm in this to win. I insist on being admired." He bent down to the dancing reptile. "We're Dutch, my dear. The Dutch are basic traders. Nothing is for free. And there has to be some profit."

Turtle slipped down his rock and waddled underneath a thorn bush.

"Not that I would mind being free of all that," the commissaris told the moving bush.

"And what was the oracle's advice today?" Katrien asked when the commissaris limped back into her kitchen.

The commissaris grinned. "I think he's holding out for more lettuce."

Chapter 4

New York received the com-
missaris pleasantly enough, after a first-class ride on the
roomy top deck of a large airplane. He had eaten, dozed
and dreamed about the hollow-eyed tram driver/angel.
The dream was probably caused by the stewardess who
served him, a tall woman with blond hair. There were
many of these in Holland now: a new archetype.

Immigration and Customs waved him through. He
didn't have to join the long line for cabs; a large burly man
in a red waistcoat guided the commissaris to a brand-new
minivan. It was illegal, of course. No hustling for rides at
Kennedy Airport. He had seen posters in the airport's
waiting areas, warning passengers.

"Isn't this illegal?" the commissaris asked the man
shooing him along.

"Been doing it for years now," the soft-spoken driver

said pleasantly enough. "Mind if I rustle up a few other passengers? It'll make the ride worthwhile. Some music while you wait? I'll give you the seat of honor."

The driver switched on his radio, tuning to a classical music station, determining his choice after a glance at the little old gentleman sitting quietly in the high passenger seat. A well-modulated male voice announced a piano concerto by Albéniz, after suggesting that listeners avail themselves of the services of an investment broker. The commissaris didn't catch the sponsor's name. The announcer interrupted after the first movement. "By the way, Gillette is a good buy today. A free tip from your favorite station. Gil-lette. A debt-free company about to launch an important new product. When the product sells, shares will go up." Music again, remarkably clear, piping in through speakers in the minivan's four corners. It died away briefly.

The announcer spoke gently: "Remember now, never wa-ger your wad."

The commissaris thought he *would* like to wager his wad now. Go for broke. All or nothing. As there was little or nothing he would be able to do with All now, victory would amount to nothing anyway. He would solve the case, retire and be forgotten. All = Zero. He thought of the reptile oracle in his Queens Avenue garden, back in Amsterdam. Turtle would agree with such radical thinking. The commissaris, feeling he was on the verge of true insight, smiled happily. Euphoric feelings floated on the lovely Albéniz composition. But he might just be ill. Flu was going around, especially within the enclosed air circulation of airplanes. He was probably infected. An oncoming fever would alter his perception.

The commissaris, shivering, paged through the police convention brochure while he laid out his plans. He would spend the rest of today in his Cavendish suite, looking down on the magnificent trees of Central Park for comfort and entertainment. Tomorrow he would attend a lecture on modes of death by Dr. Steve Russo, pathologist and assistant chief of the NYPD's Crime Laboratory, and make an appointment to meet with Detective-Sergeant Hurrell of the Central Park Precinct. For now all he had to do was lean back and listen to the music.

The driver, when he came back, herding two thirty-year-old businesswomen in suits and lace blouses, talked golf while he drove his catch into town. The commissaris watched the Manhattan skyline against an expanse of glistening blue marked by just a few little white clouds. The music was Bach now, the Italian Concerto. The announcer mentioned Gillette again.

"Make a bundle, play golf in Florida for the rest of your life," the driver was saying. He had done that for some years: long fairway shots between unusual water hazards, lagoons filled with alligators, Key West. Those were the days. But the trick was not to listen to the jokers interrupting the classical music. The driver nodded disdainfully toward his door's speaker, where the announcer had just made a suggestion.

"What does he know? Shit-eating wiseass… Oh dear, ladies present. Sorry, ladies."

The ladies were talking. They might not have heard.

"No more golf, eh?" the commissaris said.

The driver said no more golf. A bad investment on margin, lost his wad, back to a leased van, back to the merry-go-round of collecting fares to make the payments, I-owe-I-owe-off-to-the-airport-I-go, Kennedy-Manhattan-Kennedy forever.

The commissaris rembered that Katrien had mentioned a golf ball. He didn't know about sports. Of all the balls he could visualize, only the golf ball might be a weapon.

"So are you a good golf player?"

He wasn't bad, the driver said. He missed winning money and drinks at the club house. There were golf courses around New York too, but play on them was not so relaxed as in Key West, and—except for the few crowded public courses—a lot more expensive.

"Public? In parks?"

The driver, bad-tempered now, reflecting on his greed and stupidity, turned nasty although he didn't show it. He smiled at his client. "Sure, sir. In some parks."

"Now," the commissaris said, "suppose I were to be in a park, not paying attention, and I got hit with a golf ball, a good long fairway shot, as you said just now, would there be some force there? Say I got hit in the chest, for instance?"

"Kill you stone dead," the burly driver said.

So far, not so good. The commissaris felt worse when he was taken to his hotel suite. He telephoned Room Service for a pot of tea and plain cookies. He arranged his medicines: aspirins and codeine pain pills. His thermometer showed he had a fever, not too high yet. His rheumatism was definitely acting up; red-hot worms crawled about in his hipbones. The shower relaxed his body somewhat but he ended up dizzy. His throat was sore. There seemed to be crushed glass in his lungs, moving slowly every time he breathed.

He took multiple medications. While he wandered about his spacious sitting room in a cotton bathrobe, nicely ironed by Katrien, the codeine took effect. Generic acetaminophen might lower his temperature and also give pain relief. He sucked an antiseptic lozenge to reduce the sandpaper feeling in his throat, while he looked down on the tops of ash and maple and chestnut trees, admiring their full foliage. He followed birds in flight, bending sideways so he could peek at the roof of the Metropolitan Museum. He planned to visit there. De Gier had been talking about the Rockefeller wing, with its Papuan artifacts imported from New Guinea. The commissaris himself was interested in New Guinea, mainly because it seemed to be the furthest place on earth, an enormous, hardly inhabited island surrounded by exotic archipelagos.

Papua New Guinea is an island second in size only to Greenland. Much of the interior is still a vast unknown. De Gier wanted to go there "to experience primitive insights." The commissaris wouldn't mind joining the sergeant's quest. He also fantasized about trying the other side of things, even engaging in soul-testing head hunting, or ritual cannibalism perhaps. Too old, too feeble now, he dreamed about using de Gier's effort as a projection. Get the dear boy to report regularly, to write from his mystical summer camp, to provide vicarious entertainment for sickly stay-at-homes.

His phone rang. "Had a good flight, sir?"

"Yes?" the commissaris asked. "Who is this?"

"Hugh O'Neill. We're down in the lobby. Can we come up and talk about your Central Park case? I have Sergeant Hurrell with me."

The commissaris said he wasn't dressed, bit if his colleagues didn't mind...

They didn't, the hearty American voice said. But if the commissaris preferred to rest first, they could come back later.

"No, please come up."

The New York policemen seemed impressed by the luxury of the commissaris's quarters. The commissaris tried to explain. His wife was paying. He hadn't been feeling well. A present.

"But doesn't the convention take care of hotel expenses for all invitees?" Hurrell asked.

"They wouldn't pay for this," O'Neill said, noting crystal chandeliers, satin drapes, an Oriental rug on the floor, large-screen TVs and VCRs in both rooms. "Nice present. Your wife must love you." He harrumphed. "How do you want to be addressed? By rank? As Mister?" He smiled. "I'm afraid I won't be able to do your last name justice."

"Use my first name," the commissaris said. "J-a-n."

"You pronounce that as 'Yan'?"

"Any way you like. May I call you Hugh?"

"Please," O'Neill said. "First names are easy. Hurrell here is..." He seemed puzzled. "Is what?"

"Earl," Hurrell said. "Funny name. Hardly ever use it."

"Hurrell has brought his reports with him," O'Neill said.

Hurrell was a nondescript man, except for blotched cheeks and a heavily veined nose. A skin condition, the commissaris thought, or alcoholism. O'Neill was boisterous, handsome, with a full head of cropped curly auburn hair. The chief looked athletic. An American football player, the commissaris thought. Better give him the ball when he wants it before he tears you to pieces.

Both visitors were in their forties. Hurrell seemed quiet, moody, unhappy. He needed a shave. He wore a khaki windbreaker over baggy pants, with a faded red T-shirt under his jacket. O'Neill wore a good-quality suit, with the jacket unbuttoned. As the chief moved about, a holstered pistol under his armpit showed. O'Neill seemed efficient and powerful, in charge of himself, ready to take control of whatever was going on around him.

"We won't be long, Yan," O'Neill said. "You need to rest up, but the convention starts tomorrow so you might want to get your problem out of the way now. I believe the dead man is an uncle to one of your people?" He looked at his sergeant and put out a hand. Hurrell handed over a large manila envelope. O'Neill broke the seal.

The contents were shaken out on to the large coffee table. There were photographs that O'Neill sorted quickly. A map and reports were clipped together inside a plastic file.

The commissaris invited his guests to sit down. The effect of the codeine seemed to have worn off already. He felt dizzy again, O'Neill's words waving around him.

"Our dead man—Termeer, Bert—was known as a kind of an exhibitionist, maybe suffering from some compulsive disorder. Tourette's, perhaps? But he didn't expose himself, no nakedness or any such extreme behavior.

"Here is a photo of the corpse. Looks bad, doesn't he? The midsection was damaged by raccoons, we think. Oh yes, there are some living in the middle of Manhattan, in Central Park. And goddamn rats, too, the size of cats. The autopsy mentions that the eyes were pecked out by birds. Hawks will do that, and at least three species live in the park: red-tailed, sharp-shins and Cooper's hawks.

"There was also damage by seagulls, it says, but the raccoons did the big job. Dug out most of the chest and belly, tore the body in two....

"Just one night in the open. Our beastly brethren show little respect.

"Our confusion, Yan, was caused by the clothes. Termeer's body was dressed in rags when it was found. The corpse was robbed, and there must have been a clothes switch. We figured this out later. But at first we had him down as just another homeless....

"The body must have been robbed by a derelict. He would have been delighted to encounter such rich pickings: wallet, money, watch and so on....

"Little chance to trace the unknown perpetrator or perpetrators.

"We found Termeer's dentures. Quite a bit of gold in them, seems surprising the bums didn't take them... may not have seen them—azalea bushes, you know—the dentures were covered with leaves.

"Apart from the robbery, of course, no crime seems to have been committed and that was after..."

The commissaris must have asked something, although he didn't heard himself speak.

"Yes, Yan," O'Neill said. "Sure, that's where we went wrong at first. The corpse was found the next morning, you see, by kids, oh dear oh dear. And their father was with them, a medical man. The corpse was torn up, chewed by animals and pecked at—that doesn't look good in a public playground like our magnificent Central Park." O'Neill scowled at Hurrell, who was looking out of the window. "What do you have to add, Earl?"

"Right," Hurrell said. "Right, Chief. Tom and Jerry investigated. It was my day off. They might have taken note of the body's clean fingernails, the nicely cut hair, the trimmed beard and so forth. They didn't. Tom and Jerry had him zipped into a bag. They did take photographs, however."

"Tom and Jerry" sounded vaguely familiar to the commissaris. Cheery New Age faces on ice-cream lids? Cartoon characters? He smiled.

O'Neill laughed. "Hurrell's assistants. Happens to be their names. A good team, but they were sloppy here." He scowled again.

Hurrell, feeling guilty perhaps, was talking now. "Right. Eh…Yan. The mistake was that Tom and Jerry were fooled by the blanket Termeer seemed to be sleeping under." He showed the commissaris a photograph. "Filthy. See? Lots of bums sleep in the park. They're not healthy. They die. But that's no reason not to search the area. Tom and Jerry should have found the dentures but they didn't, not straight off. Maybe because they considered the subject was just another piece of garbage."

In spite of his physical misery the commissaris became aware of a silence in the room, in which Detective

Hurrell's labored breathing seemed unnaturally loud and painful.

"Okay?" O'Neill asked. "Earl? You okay?"

"Garbage…," Hurrell continued. "To be thrown out. Tom and Jerry think that way. Don't care much about fellow human beings."

There was the labored breathing again.

"Now then," Chief O'Neill said cheerfully, cutting through what was about to become more silence. "Okay. So the NYPD kinda fucked up. Happens at your end too, I'm sure. But we did get it in the end, after Charlie showed up. This Charlie was Termeer's neighbor. It's all in the report. You might care to call on him. We had the Dutch nephew by then, inquiring at the Park Precinct house. And there was that angry foreign couple, the tourists, complaining — that wasn't handled to well either." O'Neill rubbed his hair with a fist. "Things kind of piled up. But we figured it out in the end. The autopsy report was clear enough. Bizarre, though. Sergeant?"

"Yeah," Hurrell said. "The corpse was Dutch. And so was the couple who complained. But there was no connection. There must be a lot of Dutchmen around town these days."

The commissaris struggled against letting his body sag back on the couch. He thought he might be fainting. If he let on how he felt, the visitors would probably call a doctor, or, worse, an ambulance. He forced himself to appear interested. "Dutch? Dutch tourists?"

"But Termeer was alive then when the couple saw him in some sort of physical trouble," O'Neill said. "Just not feeling well, which fits in with the autopsy's findings. At that time the subject was wearing his own clothes, of course. Tweed suit. Tie. Hat. He had been gesticulating oddly and frolicking about, after standing still for a long time, finally collapsing. Older man…open-heart surgery…"

The commissaris caught on to words here and there, which came close, wafted away, turned back, floated around. He wasn't quite sure what "frolicking" meant.

O'Neill demonstrated. He held up his arms, fingers pointing at the ceiling, and skipped through the suite.

The commissaris tried to smile. "And Termeer had heart trouble, you said? Open-heart surgery? Of course, that would show on the body."

O'Neill sounded downright angry now. "Jesus F. Christ, didn't we make a mess of it though? A derelict, who'd had recent open-heart surgery? Expensive dentures in nearby bushes? Blatant contradictions. That's what police work is all about, noticing things that don't fit. It's the discrepancies that lead us to truth, right, Sergeant?" He glared. "We would still know nothing if that neighbor hadn't showed.…"

It was Hurrell talking now. Somewhat defensive. "Charlie did show and he identified the body as that of Bert Termeer, his tenant, a book dealer."

"We still had it," O'Neill said. "Good thing. Bums'

bodies don't stay around for long with our limited morgue space. They get dumped in some mass grave."

"And the Dutch couple," the commissaris said, pronouncing each word with difficulty. "The tourists."

Hurrell found a visiting card among the photographs on the table. He read aloud: "Dr. (Chemistry) Johan Lakmaker…" He read the address: Nieuwegein. "That's the town? 'Nyu-wee-jeen?'"

"But your man wasn't dead when they saw him," O'Neill said. "We have to be clear here. And when he died, much later probably, his death was from shock. The cause could have been that fat branch crashing down. Or a hard object hitting him in the chest: a ball, a rock or something. A Frisbee. The blow wasn't severe. The bruising on the skin in the chest area that remains is slight."

The commissaris tried to keep his eyes wide open. "Shock?"

"Leading to a heart attack," O'Neill said. "It doesn't matter much what the precipitant was because, whatever it was, your man wasn't murdered."

"Roughly robbed, yes," Hurrell said, "but after death. Struck by a branch. Or a random ball. No possible criminal intent here. Just happenstance, Yan, fatally connecting with a heart condition."

"Seventy years old," O'Neill was saying now. "No spring chicken. All that running around the park, and then standing still, posing like some silly statue. Your man was asking for trouble."

"Happenstance," the commissaris repeated. He liked that word.

"You look all worn out," O'Neill said kindly. "We'll leave you our paperwork. It should be self-explanatory. Look it over sometime. No hurry. Here is my card. Phone me if you have questions. Get some sleep first. I'll have you picked up for the lecture tomorrow. It's my pal Russo's show, right? On modes of death or something? Russo will be all gung ho about Maggotmaid again. You will like that."

"Maggotmaid?"

O'Neill raised a joking finger. "Surprise, Yan. You'll find out tomorrow."

Hurrell was doing his heavy breathing again.

"Ball," the commissaris said. "People play ball in your park. Like what kind of ball? Golf?"

"Baseball—softball—volleyball maybe, soccer, lacrosse," O'Neill said. "I used to play that. Used to be an Indian sport. A pretty rough game. They still play lacrosse in the park, Hurrell?"

"Some," Hurrell said. "We don't want them to, but it happens. Ball games are restricted to a few clearly marked areas. Park personnel are supposed to warn offenders. But there are always the assholes."

The commissaris hadn't been able to concentrate. He was feeling nauseous too. So lacrosse was some kind of

Indian golf? And there were illegal ball games played in the park? He felt too sick to ask for details.

The commissaris, surprisingly, found himself on his feet, guiding his guests to the suite's door, pumping their hands, thanking them. Excusing himself again for wearing his pajamas and bathrobe.

The burst of energy didn't last. He had trouble making it to his four-poster, where he collapsed, groaned and thrashed about for a while, before getting up to stumble about the suite's bathroom, looking for more medication.

Chapter 5

"I like this little town of Nieuwegein," Adjutant Grijpstra said, after he had switched off the car engine. "How pleasant to get out of Amsterdam sometimes. We can even park here, Rinus. No pollution. Look at those huge trees. If those screeching magpies would shut up it would be real peaceful."

The unmarked police car stood in a private parking lot belonging to a row of new town houses overlooking the river Rhine. The houses showed their forbidding backsides to the detectives, and further hid behind a raised row of new brick planters containing baby evergreen bushes that would grow into more protection later.

Grijpstra read the note Sergeant de Gier passed him. "Lakmaker, Joop and Sara. They're the Central Park witnesses we are after?"

De Gier had given up trying to figure out how to

fold the road map. He now flattened it with his fist. In spite of the long drive his mood was still good. He had followed Grijpstra's order: Gridlocked speedways had been avoided. The journey from Amsterdam had followed tree-lined canal quays and dikes twisting along narrow rivers. De Gier had pointed at fishermen in rowboats, sitting quietly behind their rods, at storks and herons planing on breezes, at turning windmills.

"Beautiful," Grijpstra said each time. "Lovely country. Nice spring we're having."

"I don't like this," Grijpstra said now. "Interviewing stale witnesses. How did Lakmaker strike you when you phoned for the appointment?"

"Member of the elderly arrogant class," de Gier said. "Old coot with a university background. Enjoys an ample pension. Addressed me as 'policeman.'"

Grijpstra grinned. "Maybe we'll end up with a cigar each, to put beneath our caps."

"You do the talking," de Gier said. "I'm allergic to their kind."

Grijpstra didn't move yet; they had arrived early.

De Gier looked at the town houses' unfriendly backsides. "Two hundred thousand each?"

Grijpstra thought the town houses would price at three. One hundred thousand extra for the view of the Rhine.

De Gier kept staring while he wondered how the old couple would live, while viewing Holland's widest, most splendid river. So what else do you do? Ignore the aching old body while watching boats sail through your picture windows?

Discipline yourself? One hour of viewing, ten minutes for checking *TV GUIDE* for nature programs later on? Nap? Dinner? De Gier asked Grijpstra.

"NEWS!" Grijpstra shouted.

"WHAT?"

Grijpstra pointed out that de Gier didn't have to shout in his face. Grijpstra had merely acted out how an elderly couple conducts dialogue. One sees a newscaster clearing his throat and shouts at the other to come watch the news. Or vice versa. Then, while one partner makes hurry-up movements, the other comes hobbling along so that the complete couple can share Worldly Horrors.

De Gier had trouble imagining the scene.

"Sharing of media-fodder," Grijpstra said. He also suggested membership in a chess club or a bird-watching society: Identified species can be crossed off a list. Or visiting even older elderly persons in institutions. The couple might also invent ways to improve life on the planet.

De Gier got it now. He suggested guilt. The old couple analyzes past mistakes. They fantasize about how things could have been better. They prepare for a painless end by studying euthanasia literature supplied by their doctor.

"Read the *Rotterdam Times* and quote from same?"

de Gier asked. He tried to vocalize the *Rotterdam Times*'s style of reporting, hardly opening his lips, keeping his nose closed, expressing wise-ass opinions in the latest clichés.

"Okay, okay," Grijpstra said, "it's still my paper. Only the *Rotterdam Times* dares to mention police corruption."

"You subscribe?" de Gier asked.

Grijpstra sometimes read the paper at Café Keyzer, Fridays, between mocha cake and espresso.

"The photographs are okay," de Gier said. "Politicians all look like compulsive jerk-offs, schizoid too."

"That one old drunk looked handsome, can't think of his name now."

De Gier agreed that Holland's vice president was rather photogenic.

It was about time now.

De Gier looked at macramé curtains covering the glass part of the Lakmaker front door.

Grijpstra reread the commissaris's faxed note: *Find out what exactly the Lakmakers saw on June 4.* Grijpstra checked the day on his watch. "Almost three weeks ago." *Ask* (the note ordered) *why they ignored Sergeant Hurrell's queries left on their answering machine.*

"Are we going to interrogate the Lakmakers separately?" de Gier asked. "In different rooms? Catch them later on all the discrepancies?"

Grijpstra didn't think so. "Might annoy them too much."

"They're annoyed already," de Gier said.

"Angry, well-meaning fellow citizens," Grijpstra said. "But don't they have a nice place to live in?" He pushed his car door open. "I attack, Sergeant. Follow me."

Grijpstra and de Gier sat on a couch upholstered in blue velvet and drank coffee from Chinese mugs adorned with hand-painted flowers. A limping white-haired old lady pointed at cargo vessels motoring along the Rhine. Her bald husband checked a plastic file on his desk. It contained maps and leaflets, mementos of the couple's recent American journey.

"That couch you two are sitting on is original Biedermeier," Sara Lakmaker said. "A wreck when I found it. Joop repaired the frame and I upholstered it. It would cost a fortune if you figured in the hours."

"The professional artistic touch," Grijpstra said. He moved carefully, anxious not to damage the couch's ancient springs, which creaked painfully under his bulk.

"The coffee you are drinking comes from Nigeria," Sara said. "It's from Zabar's, in New York. That's the biggest and best deli in the world. In New York you can buy anything. Americans still have the greatest buying power."

"A strong and interesting flavor," Grijpstra said.

"Care to join me here?" Joop Lakmaker asked from his desk. He had unfolded a map. "This is Central Park and this is where we saw the man you are inquiring about now. Just off this path, next to that meadow." Lakmaker changed both his voice and his posture so that he could be a poet, speaking loudly and with a rhetorical effect. "The grass was green," Lakmaker declaimed, "and the gent was dying. The balloon beast was rising"—Lakmaker covered his heart with his hand—"and the children were playing." He looked at Grijpstra. "How does that sound?"

"That sounds real pretty," Grijpstra said.

Lakmaker grinned. "I didn't even have to put in the blooming azaleas. I wanted to be a poet, wear a corduroy suit, live in a mountain cabin, but Sara wanted us to live usefully instead."

"Joop," Sara warned.

"And usefully we lived. A lifetime long. Do you know," Joop asked, "that I was instrumental in lowering the cost of Dutch soda pop?" Joop's bulging eyes looked through Grijpstra. "Isn't that something?"

"You were much appreciated," Sara said. "You did a good job. You raised good kids." Sara smiled. "You collected art." She pointed at three masks hung above the large TV screen. "We already auctioned off two collections and now Joop has started collecting again. Impressive? They are Bolivian. We bought them on a trip. Mine workers make them from beer cans during their yearly holiday."

Grijpstra and de Gier looked at the masks. "Devils?"

"Mine demons," Sara said. "They live underground and come up with the workers, to share their holiday."

The masks sprouted blunt horns, and blood dripped from the eyes.

"Expressive," Grijpstra said.

"I changed my interests and collected Fellini." Joop pointed at stacked videotapes. "I want that included in my obituary."

"Joop," Sara warned.

"Not in the *Rotterdam Times*," Joop said, "I know I'm not on that level. Maybe in the *Nieuwegein Advertiser*?" He was rubbing his hands. "What do you think, policeman? You think that my regression from present-day pop art to a nostalgic interest in surrealism, due to reliving World War II horrors, will make good copy?"

"So that poor old man in Central Park was Dutch," Sara said. "He spoke English to us. Amazing. Our running into a Dutchman in Central Park, I mean."

"Nothing out-of-the-way about that," Joop said. "Holland is rich so we Dutch can travel. New York welcomes big spenders. Six jumbos a day on the transatlantic route. 'Step right up, step right up.'" He made inviting gestures. "We're bound to stumble into each other in Central Park."

"Did that poor man survive?" Sara asked. "He seemed to be feeling very bad. The horse kicked him, you know. There he was, spinning and turning. And that uniformed hussy just rode off."

"Uniformed hussy," Grijpstra said. "What uniformed hussy would that be?"

"The policewoman," Sara said. "We had been watching the poor man for a while, you see. So had she. From high up on her huge horse."

"Well," Joop said, "that's what you *thought*, Sara. We can't know for sure. She was wearing sunglasses."

"To answer your question," Grijpstra said, "yes, the old man died. He was found in the azalea bushes the next morning. So the police horse kicked him?"

"Just a little," Sara said. "There was a lot going on. They had a big balloon beast going up for the kids, on the meadow, some kind of dinosaur."

"Tyrannosaurus rex," Joop said. "Enormous. Made from multicolor balloons stuck together."

"And there was a jazz group playing, on a big bandstand."

"Don't underestimate jazz," said Joop. "Even if I collect classical myself I admit that jazz is a superior art form." He looked at de Gier.

De Gier nodded.

"We had been listening to the music," Sara said. "And watching all the costumed people. There was a contest going on. Look-alikes of famous movie characters. Madonna in garters. Monroe pretending her skirt was caught in a draft. Marlon Brando dancing the last tango. Yves Montand being seduced by Catherine Deneuve."

"Mayor Koch was one of the judges," Joop said. "Odd-looking man but his speech was funny."

"But this man you came about," Sara said. "He was

the most impressive. He reminded me of a professor I had when I was studying interior decoration in Utrecht."

"He wasn't part of the contest, was he?"

Sara seemed sure. "Oh no, not at all."

"I can see you are an interior decorator, that you are visually perceptive," Grijpstra said, looking about the apartment, noting open spaces and a different way of lighting. "Could you describe the man, please?"

"A tall majestic old man wearing plus fours," Sara said. "Like mountaineers do. Old-fashioned trousers that tie up half-way between knee and ankle. And a waistcoat and jacket, all dark brown tweed, a matching outfit. White shirt, buttoned down. Plaid tie. Long white beard. High forehead. Sharp nose. Bushy eyebrows. Lovely blue eyes. Polished boots and cream woolen stockings. A full head of hair."

"Sara loves hairy types," Joop said. "He struck me as a performer. He was standing absolutely still when Sara first saw him, but I had noticed the fellow before. He was skipping about then, an unlikely thing for a sage to do."

"Where was I," Sara asked, "when he skipped?"

"Going kootchy-coo at a baby."

"A sage?" Grijpstra asked.

"A kind of Voltaire type. You've heard of Voltaire?" Joop asked. "He had that sort of world-waking aura, but he looked rather like George Bernard Shaw. You've heard of George Bernard Shaw?"

Grijpstra looked at de Gier.

De Gier nodded.

"Yes," Grijpstra said. "He looked like them, did he?"

"Upper-class prophet," Sara said. "That's what he seemed like to me. Not crazy looking, but decent. After the skipping he stood at a crossing—still, like a statue, on one leg, leaning forward. Posing, in an exaggerated attitude, for effect. Very startling. You couldn't help noticing the man, and wondering what he was up to."

"Kids went over and touched him," Joop said. "Making sure he was real." He nodded. "Excellent performer. A showman. You know?"

"And then we became aware of the mounted cop, also watching him," Sara said. "Mounted cops look nice in America. Not operatic-looking, like here. No long coats and stupid hats. In America their wear blue helmets. And that policewoman had a long ponytail. She wore a smart uniform. Dark riding pants, a blue starched shirt. A lot of leather. High boots. Belt."

"Nice-Nazi," Joop said. "Gun belt with hardware, complete, all the sidearms and a two-way radio with waving antenna. Like in *Star Wars*. I liked those films," Joop said. "I don't like the police myself, of course. They're all fascists, you know. Will do anything when ordered. Like in the war when they picked up my parents. Dutch cops did that, because the Germans said to take all Jews to the railway station. If I hadn't been playing outside they would have kicked me into a boxcar too. To gas me in Treblinka."

"Yes," Grijpstra said.

"Nothing personal," Joop said. "Obedience to authority goes with being human. We like to follow orders. Gets us up in the morning. We like violence too. Now there are Jewish police on the West Bank and in Gaza. Doing the same thing. Then that will turn around and they'll be beating us up again." Joop smiled, impressed with the exactitude of his argument. "Maybe humanity can evolve though? Suddenly twist its genes and become a new species?"

"Joop," Sara warned.

"So the Central Park female police officer on horseback caused her mount to kick Termeer?" Grijpstra asked. "That was his name, by the way, the name of the man you call a prophet. She attacked Bert Termeer, using her horse as a weapon?"

"No," Joop said. "That's to say, not on purpose. This Termeer was standing still, like a statue of someone, about to take off at speed, and then suddenly he did. He leaped onto the path, to start skipping again—the other part of his act—and the horse reared and its hoof struck him."

"The policewoman ignored that?" Grijpstra asked. "She rode off? Left the scene of an accident without taking proper action?"

"No," Sara said. "She dismounted and asked him if he was okay. He said he was, and then she rode off. But he wasn't okay. Soon after that the man—Mr. Termeer—started reeling and swaying. We helped him over to a bench. The policewoman was still in view, riding about in the meadow where the people were bopping to jazz from the bandstand. When we started yelling and waving, she came back and got nasty."

"Ordered us 'on our way,'" Joop said. "We're not the kind of people that can be ordered around, you know. We complained about her. Left our card at the Park Precinct."

"Of course," Sara said, "we didn't expect to get any response."

"You didn't get the messages the NYPD left on your machine?" Grijpstra said.

Sara blushed.

"Before we went on our trip I bought a new answering machine," Joop said. "When we came home Sara pressed the wrong button and erased everything. So this gentleman—Termeer—died, did he? What of, do you know?"

"Maybe a heart attack," Grijpstra said. "The body was found in some azalea bushes, dressed in rags, partly covered by a filthy blanket. Animals had consumed some of the corpse. Mr. Termeer's dentures were found at a distance from the body." The adjutant produced the faxed NYPD report and accompanying photograph, which had come through fairly clearly. Then he folded the papers and put the photo back in his inside jacket pocket. "I don't think you want to see this."

Joop was quiet. Sara poured more coffee.

"Termeer wasn't having a heart attack," Joop said while he passed around nonpareils. "Not when we saw him. I have had two heart attacks myself. He didn't seem to have a headache, wasn't feeling his neck, there was nothing wrong with his left arm, none of the well-known symptoms. He was just dazed, but after we helped him sit down I'm sure he felt much better."

"Were there any other people around?" Grijpstra asked.

Nobody. By then, both Lakmakers stated, events in the meadow were in full swing: The balloon dinosaur was being launched, the jazz band was playing.

"'When the Saints Go Marching In,'" Joop said.

The look-alikes and wannabes were lining up for their contest. There was nobody else at the crossing where Termeer, cared for by the Lakmaker couple, was recuperating from shock.

Grijpstra seemed ready to leave the Lakmakers' residence when de Gier took over. "Why," he asked Joop, "did you pay so much attention to this, this George Bernard Shaw type?"

"You don't know about George Bernard Shaw," Joop said. "How could you, policeman? What is your rank?"

"Yes," Grijpstra looked at de Gier. "George Bernard Who?"

Grijpstra looked at Joop. "De Gier is a sergeant."

"The sergeant reads a lot," Grijpstra told Sara.

"Without using dictionaries. It takes him a few years to pick up a language. He likes languages, you see."

"You graduated from a grammar school?" Joop asked de Gier. "Wouldn't that qualify you for academic study? Shouldn't you be an inspector then, or a lieutenant or something?"

It took a while for de Gier to get the witnesses to confirm that Termeer had made an extraordinary impression. It wasn't just being good Samaritans, for they weren't, both Sara and Joop admitted. In New York they had stepped over homeless people, ignored beggars, walked away from traffic accidents. And it wasn't just New York—they would do that anywhere. At the most they would "alert the authorities," but the authorities, in Termeer's case, were right there. So when Bert Termeer was sent reeling by the policewoman's horse, the couple interfered for other reasons.

"Because you were upset with the authorities?" de Gier asked.

Joop was willing to go along with that, as an easy way out, but Sara said she wanted to be honest.

The interrogation continued. Honest is nice. De Gier was smiling at Sara. He liked her.

"No," Sara confessed. Now that she was old and retired and more able to watch the human situation *as is* she no longer felt much pity. Her sense of duty was way down too. If a man gets hurt by the police there is little one can do. She did do that little, by complaining about the policewoman at the Central Park Precinct, but normally she wouldn't have done that either. Certainly not in America where she happened to be as a tourist.

So what was abnormal? Why did Sara Lakmaker involve herself with a man she had already called prophet-like, philosopher-like, Shaw- and/or Voltaire-like....

"Who is Voltaire?" Grijpstra asked de Gier. "One of your nihilists again?"

De Gier didn't think so. "Voltaire insisted on being rich; it guaranteed his independence."

"A benevolent atheist," Joop said, "who abhorred useless punishment."

"The sergeant likes the idea of Nothing," Grijpstra told the Lakmakers. "He lives in an empty apartment and he doesn't have a car. He does buy clothes, though. Has them made. But he doesn't have many."

"Are you married?" Joop asked de Gier.

"He is not," Grijpstra said.

"Ever been married?"

"That wouldn't be consistent with his insight, would it now?" Grijpstra asked.

"You have a dog?"

"He lives with a cat," Grijpstra said.

"You really have no car?"

"Never," Grijpstra said.

"I did own an orange Deux Chevaux once," de Gier said, "but it was stolen."

"But he doesn't have a TV," Grijpstra said.

"And he doesn't talk much," Joop told his wife. "The fat policeman does that for him."

Grijpstra looked at Joop.

"Portly," Joop said, patting his own protruding stomach. "I am sorry, policeman."

"Joop," warned Sara.

"So you like the idea of Nothing?" Joop asked de Gier. "You want to own Nothing or you want to be Nothing?"

De Gier was still chewing on his nonpareil.

"The sergeant wants to be Nothing," Grijpstra said. "But he can't tell you that because then he makes Something out of Nothing. We often discuss that apparent controversy. I always get tangled up."

"You would," Joop said.

"Joop," Sara warned.

"I'm sorry," Joop said. He smiled apologetically. "I would like to belong to Nothing too. That's why I refused to wear a star as a kid, even in spite of my parents, who said that I should, because the German Nazis were It then, and if It tells you to wear a star then you do that. But I didn't so I was Nothing, and I was playing outside, and that's why I am still Something today."

"So," de Gier said, "you felt attracted to this Bert Termeer, the man who was found in rags in Central Park, partly eaten by animals, under a filthy blanket."

"He seemed like a kind of prophet," Sara Lakmaker said.

"You like prophets?"

Sara did.

Perhaps, Grijpstra suggested on the way home to Amsterdam, with rain slapping against the windscreen, Sara had prolonged the interview because she felt attracted to handsome de Gier. Maybe Sara didn't want the sergeant to go as yet. De Gier shrugged that away. "Why not allow Mrs. Lakmaker to be nice?"

Grijpstra wouldn't do that.

Chapter 6

The commissaris didn't have a good night physically, although mentally he qualified the episode as exciting. He was up a lot, with bathroom problems. He kept his headache down with the generic painkiller. He drank his cold tea, wondered whether he should disturb Room Service, emptied out the nonalcoholic contents of his small refrigerator. He did get some sleep but the long-legged streetcar driver kept appearing. In spite of what he had told Katrien, the recurring dream had definite sexual aspects, although he hardly felt aroused. The Angel of Death's hollow eye sockets might have put him off. He whimpered himself awake, tried to remember the dream's details, but they mostly slipped away. Frustrated, he found himself padding about barefoot on the thick Oriental carpet, hoping for daylight. Stopping at the suite's picture windows he could see shadowy figures moving in the park below, derelicts searching garbage cans for food. He told himself things could be worse, got back into bed and drank more soda.

He got up at nine o'clock; the "Modes of Death" lecture wasn't till eleven. The Cavendish's breakfast room was inviting enough, with a complete buffet, the fragrance of fresh rolls, a display of smoked fish, flowers everywhere, a marble fountain sprinkling in a corner, but he went out anyway, clasping his cane. A walk would do him good. He limped along, the pain in his hipbones dulled by codeine.

Thrushes sang as he found a restaurant off Madison Avenue, Le Chat Complet. He was feeling bad again. The restaurant occupied a basement with high narrow windows. Three tall black men with shaven skulls, wearing identical red jackets and red butterfly ties on impeccable white shirts, busied themselves behind the counter. They hummed as they filled orders shouted by waitresses darting about between the tables. The feet of passersby were visible in the high windows, occasionally the feet and legs of dogs. When a complete cat showed itself the cooks broke out into song.

"Le chat complet…"

There was also instrumentation: percussion on cowbells and what sounded like a sock cymbal, hidden under the counter. One of the cooks, in between breaking eggs and spearing sausages, played the xylophone on a row of labelless bottles.

The commissaris, waiting for his order of French

toast and bacon, a menu item discovered during a previous visit to the USA (he also asked for fries, a potato dish he had tried to get Katrien to make, but she couldn't), compared the model in a painting with a little old lady bustling about the restaurant. The painting, three by four feet, dominated the cellar. It showed a naked black woman, in her thirties, with large firm breasts, reclining on a cane couch under palm trees. The woman was about to bite into a red apple. A black dog stared up at her. A blood red tongue lolled out of the dog's mouth. There were purple mountains in the background of the painting.

The commissaris was sure the old lady refilling coffee cups all over the restaurant was an older version of the luscious woman in the painting. Even in her white apron and red butterfly necktie she showed the same immoral attitude, an irresistible abandon, as in her earlier projection. He wondered where the painted scene was set.

"Haiti," the little old lady said when she came by to check his tea. "We from Haiti. The country. *La campagne.*" She bent down to peer at his cup. "What you do to your tea?"

The painting had required all the concentration he had been able to muster for he had put both lemon and milk in his tea. The resulting fluid curdled in his mug.

"Stupide," the woman said. "Mamère bring you fresh tea. No charge. Because this my restaurant and you are *stupide.*"

The commissaris took his time over breakfast. The

cellar filled up and he had to share his table. He hoped that another cat would set off the jazzy musical he had enjoyed before. No cat showed.

An unmarked police car driven by Sergeant Hurrell picked him up at the Cavendish and dropped him off at One Police Plaza in what, considering the distance and heavy traffic, seemed a surprisingly short time. Hurrell, who had guided the commissaris into the rear seat of the car, evidently wasn't looking for talkative company. He drove silently, scowling at black or turbaned cab drivers who wiggled fingers at him and smiled. Apparently there was a way for the drivers to recognize Hurrell's car as police. The commissaris cleared his throat and was about to ask for an explanation when Hurrell looked at his passenger via his mirror. "It's the type of antennae we use. Or maybe they can smell me."

In the reception hall there were speeches and coffee. The commissaris recognized colleagues from European countries. He waved and shook hands. German heels clicked. French hands flourished. A British detective chief smiled affably. Only the American hosts wore uniforms.

Dr. Russo was a handsome slim man who looked like he worked out regularly. His lecture was enthusiastic. Gory slides illustrated his subjects. The first slide showed a skull with a ragged hole in it. Russo explained that the human remnant was found in a pit dug to hold pillars that would support yet another super-tall building. The hole indicated foul play. "Someone bashed our friend," Russo said happily, "but he did so a very long time ago. My guess is four hundred years. We found other skulls nearby—keepsakes dating back to Indian executions."

There was the same picture, but now in color, and showing more detail, that the commissaris had faxed to his assistants in Amsterdam and that Adjutant Grijpstra, after deliberation, had not shown to Sara. The commissaris, studying the way the Central Park animals had consumed all of the belly, the genitals and part of the upper thighs, reflected on the unacceptability of identifying human existence with the body. Could this mess be what we are?

"Bodies definitely don't last."

He had said so aloud and an Oriental man sitting next to him, an official from Seattle, nodded agreement. "We had the same thing in a wooded area right next to a suburb. Just one night and pffftt...hardly enough for identification."

"Heart attack in Central Park," Dr. Russo said brightly. "A crowd of a thousand people probably within shouting distance. This man must have fallen down and crawled about for a bit, ending up under flowering azalea bushes. There is some evidence that he was hit in the chest, possibly by a rotten branch. He was under a maple that had been struck by lightning a long time ago. A branch was torn off by strong winds that night. Subsequent research and inquiries reveal that subject was well dressed and nicely groomed when the heart attack occurred. At some time he was found and robbed, probably by homeless people, judging from the clothes swap. Maybe his feet stuck out of the bushes then. We found some signs that the body had been dragged further into the underbrush."

The pathologist clicked a dozen slides through his machine. Some slides showed the body remains from different angles. One slide focused on Termeer's beard. The dentures were shown. "Classy," Dr. Russo said. "There is gold in those dentures. They were found at some distance from the other remains."

The commissaris raised his hand. "How far away from the corpse, Doctor, please?"

Russo checked his notes. "Four feet from the body."

"Do you have prints from the robbers' feet?"

"No," Russo said. "I was hoping for that but there was too much disturbance. The animal tracks blotted out all human prints. The feeding frenzy must have made the varmints hyperactive. Pity. Human footprints can be conclusively identified." He shook his head. "But we could get no clear impressions." He looked at the commissaris. "You have a special interest, sir?"

The commissaris said he was looking into a complaint.

"I remember," Dr. Russo said. "Chief O'Neill mentioned you. You're from Amsterdam, right? Call my office anytime, we'll be happy to be of assistance. I think we can reassure your complainant that the unfortunate incident was an act of God or rather"—Dr. Russo smiled—"an unfortunate combination of a number of divine doings."

The audience laughed, like a taped background on a sitcom, the commissaris thought, as he found himself smiling assent politely.

The Seattle policeman spoke up. "Couldn't it be that whoever took the subject's clothes and possessions murdered him first?"

"Aggravated or even caused the heart attack by pushing the victim around, you suggest?" Russo said. "But there would have been no need. I can't show you all the scars of the bypass operation, because part of the chest area is missing, but the marks are there. We also have testimony from a neighbor that the subject was operated on within the last two years and told to take it easy. It seem that he did not do so. We have reports of the man running about the park."

"Thank you," the Seattle chief said.

"A subtle point," Russo said. "Morally, of course, we can argue that manhandling a dying person is a criminal act, especially when the activity involves robbing that person, but in such an instance it's hard to come up with a charge of murder."

"Suspect will say that he thought the victim was drunk," a voice said.

"Criminal negligence or recklessness," another voice said, "very hard to make that stand up in court."

"We have no suspects," a voice, which the commissaris recognized as O'Neill's, said clearly. "Whoever robbed the victim is now hidden somewhere in a shelter. We tried but it would take too many hours to check all the homeless people in Manhattan."

"More questions?" Dr. Russo asked. "No? Then let me tell you about Maggotmaid."

"The commissaris's leg pains had come back in full strength but he forced himself to listen to Dr. Russo's lecture, knowing that the pain would be reduced to an inconsequential throb for as long as he could keep his mind focused on another subject.

The slide shown was the cover picture of the leaflet that had announced this police convention in New York. It showed the still, dead face of a young attractive woman. The slide was in full color. A white substance showed in the corners of the mouth. Spittle? No. Maggots. Russo seemed to take professional pleasure in clicking on other slides, magnifications of the whiteness. Each slide's higher magnification made clearer that the audience was looking at living matter: crawling maggots.

"The gal was found in the trunk of a brand-new Cadillac, parked in the hot sun in front of a deli."

The police chiefs listened as the pathologist enthusiastically described the smell of rotten flesh wafting steadily from the luxury automobile. The deli's owners, concerned about their business—their store window showed a display of choice meats—alerted the police. Uniformed officers forced the trunk with a crowbar.

People gasped when they saw a dead female human body, soon to be known as "Maggotmaid," stretched out in the car's ample trunk. There were no signs of violence but small pieces of broken glass and wood splinters were found in the dead woman's clothing during a painstaking investigation by forensic criminologists. Meanwhile, detectives traced the owner of the Cadillac, a vehicle with Texas license plates, to a nearby Upper West Side apartment. The subject, described by Russo as a Texan named Trevor, claimed ignorance. Yes, he vaguely knew the woman, a prostitute who could be picked up in Central Park, but he hadn't invited her to that weekend's party.

"But," the detectives said, "she was there." Splinters and glass matched a broken door inside the apartment. Trevor proposed that if Maggotmaid had been at the apartment rented in his name, a guest, friend or associate—a gate-crasher maybe?—might have brought her in. Any of Trevor's friends had access to his car keys. The keys hung in the apartment's hall. Several of his associates took turns changing the vehicle's parking spot, in obedience to alternate-side-of-the-street parking rules in the neighborhood. These associates also fed the parking meters, which would explain why the vehicle hadn't been towed away by traffic policemen. None of these associates happened to be around right then, but they did show up later. They confirmed having moved the Cadillac around and fed parking meters with coins. Nobody remembered having put Maggotmaid in the Caddy's trunk. Nobody had smelled the body. Which could be true, Dr. Russo said. Tests indicated that Maggotmaid had died during a Saturday night. She was found Wednesday afternoon, when the weather suddenly changed from fairly cool to hot. The Cadillac had been baking in the sun all that day.

"Maggotmaid died of an overdose of heroin," Russo said. "We ascertained that much. We also found that her body had penetrated a glass door in Trevor's apartment. Did she fall? Was she pushed?" He wobbled his eyebrows. "A small quantity of heroin was found in the main sitting room. There were a few grams of cannabis products here and there, and many empty bottles. Trevor claimed to have no knowledge of any drug use. Nobody came forward to admit ownership of the heroin and cannabis products."

There were questions.

No, no arrests had been made, Dr. Russo said, but the investigation was still ongoing. He checked his notes. "Under the guidance of Detective-Sergeant Earl Hurrell, assisted by Detectives-First-Class Tom Tierney and Jerry Curran."

Yes, Trevor was a suspected dealer of note, allegedly in charge of several retail salesmen who worked the park.

Had investigators come up with a theory so far? Well, it was quite simple. Maggotmaid had been brought in to entertain Trevor's guests. She overdosed and died. A dead body does little to improve a party. Trevor, or an associate, probably stoned and/or drunk, had carried the body down and dumped it in the Cadillac's trunk for the meantime. There must have been a plan to get rid of the body later, which wouldn't have been a big deal—there are the rivers, there is Central Park—but, as the partying went on, Maggotmaid was forgotten.

After the lecture the commissaris attended a luncheon offered by the NYPD to its distinguished guests and colleagues. He kept shivering through the speeches and toasts. He was reasonably sure he was running a high temperature. He felt faint. It seemed his glasses had fogged up again, which was strange for he had just blown and spat on them and rubbed them clean with his necktie.

"You look tired," O'Neill's voice said. "I'll drive you to the Cavendish. Tomorrow's lecture is by a bigwig from the Los Angeles County Sheriff's Crime Laboratory on physical evidence relating to hit and run cases." O'Neill's elbow nudged the commissaris's arm. "I hear you have more cars in Holland now than there are in all of Africa. Five million cars in such a small country." O'Neill whistled admiringly. "Hit and run must be a common occurrence there. I'm sure your comments will be worth hearing tomorrow."

Chapter 7

The query the commissaris faxed off late that afternoon from the Cavendish desk, before consuming the hotel's nouvelle cuisine dinner specials, caused surprise in Amsterdam Police Headquarters.

Detective-Constable Simon Cardozo, a curly-haired young man in a rumpled corduroy suit, brought the fax in and, when he was unable to attract attention, jumped up and down while he read its text loudly.

He shouted the word "GOLF."

Grijpstra had been practicing on a set of drums, which, for years, had been kept in his office, as Lost & Found was desperately short of space and had no idea where the set had come from. De Gier provided background on his dented mini trumpet. They were trying out a composition by the Dutch group Chazz called *Water-*

straat Blue, with a young black student detective pecking out the melody on a small Yamaha keyboard, confiscated by Cardozo from an unmusical street musician using too powerful amplification. Cardozo, it turned out soon enough, could not learn to play the instrument either.

"Golf?" Adjutant Grijpstra asked after he had studied the commissaris's note. "Are we to believe that Termeer was knocked down, maybe even killed by a *golf* ball, in a public park, for God's sake?" He studied the commissaris's note again. "And what, please, is *lacrosse*?"

Cardozo knew. He had seen the game played on TV. Early Native Americans—using long-handled racketlike implements, "crosses," to hit a hard little deerskin ball—considered lacrosse as combat training. "A rough sport," Cardozo said, "with thousands of players on each side, with goals miles apart." Players got wounded, even killed. The white man changed the rules, making the game soft, with only twelve players on each side and penalties for "unnecessary roughness." But it was still a bruising sport.

"The ball," Cardozo said, "is now hard rubber."

"And it could have knocked down our man," Grijpstra said. "Oh dear."

"And what are we to do?" de Gier asked.

The commissaris's note said that they were to ask the chief-constable, who played golf, to locate an expert, and to consult with same.

Grijpstra and de Gier were received by the owner of

the Crailo Golf Club, some thirty miles out of Amsterdam. Balder Gudde, former golf champion, dressed in a sky blue suit, could have modeled for a semitransparent figure in a Magritte painting.

"A good day to you," Grijpstra said, pocketing his police identification, which Baldert tried to study while he held the plastic-laminated card upside down. "Just a few questions if you please. Merely routine. My colleague and I are interested in a possible deadly impact caused by a golf ball."

"At this golf club?" Baldert asked nervously.

"Anywhere," Grijpstra said.

"Not specifically here?" Baldert asked. "No. Could have been here, though. Right? In fact, you *do* mean here." He stepped back, sideways, forward, sideways. "Out with it, Detective, are you treating me as a suspect?"

"As an expert," Grijpstra said. "This isn't our jurisdiction, sir."

From Baldert's babbling the detectives gradually understood that they were accused of looking into the death of Baron Hilger van Hopper at the Crailo Golf Club. The baron had been a star member of Baldert's establishment. He wasn't anymore because he had passed away, just a few weeks ago. Baldert winked, reminding the detectives jokingly—as if they didn't know all about the dead baron—that the baron had died at his own so-called wedding party.

"You don't say," Grijpstra said.

Baldert kept winking.

De Gier thought he would humor the golfer, who might suffer from a disorder. "What did the baron die of, sir?"

Baldert shrugged. Then he mimed swinging a golf club.

"Overextended himself?" Baldert asked Grijpstra. "Physical shock? A golf ball whizzing by too close for comfort?" He patted Grijpstra's arm. "But you know all that, Detective. I told the lieutenant. Want to go through all that again?"

Grijpstra checked his watch. Nellie was cooking mussel soup that evening. He liked mussel soup, especially when it was made Nellie's way, with mustard and shallots. De Gier checked his watch too. A musical group from Papua New Guinea was to perform that night at Amsterdam's Tropical Museum. Spectacular cassowary-bone-rattle percussion was their forte. The leaflet said that listeners had been known to enjoy remarkable insights.

"As you know," Baldert said in his unlikely falsetto, while waddling ahead, flapping his arms as he led the way across a field, "as you must have been told by the Rijkspolitie lieutenant, Detectives, the baron died in the pavilion over there."

"What we wanted to ask you...," Grijpstra said.

"I was practicing at the time," Baldert said. "I was a bit bored. We had over two hundred guests but they were watching plastic ducks. Way over around the pond there. A race by windup ducks. The guests were betting money. I was over there, out of sight of the guests. I may have to arrange them, but duck races bore me. The baron was too drunk and too stoned to leave the pavilion. He usually was. Maybe I had been drinking some. So I could have directed my drive toward the pavilion. Even if I did, the ball missed the baron."

Grijpstra put a heavy hand on Baldert's shoulder. "Could a golf ball driven by an expert golf player have killed this baron?"

"It didn't." Baldert's eyes bulged. "The autopsy proved that."

De Gier strolled along, his tall body at ease, but the tips of his huge mustache quivered. He kept his voice down. "But the ball you hit *could* have killed your friend?"

"Extreme wear and tear killed the baron," Baldert said. "Isn't that what the autopsy came up with? Heart? A seventy-year-old man who indulged continuously? The baron liked to dip his Cubans into a double jenever and suck the alcohol through the tobacco. His liver was bad. He was coked up too. He had sinus trouble. He had been overeating at the party. And the twins, those active fellows, his 'Javanese princes,' as he called them..."

"Twins?"

"Double gay mock marriage," Baldert said. "That's why we had the party."

De Gier nodded as if it all made perfect sense. "And

you hit that tee shot. Did anyone see you?"

Baldert, leading the way back to his office, insisted, "It didn't strike the baron."

"But if it had hit him," de Gier asked, "in the chest, for instance?"

Baldert sweated.

"Yes, Baldert?"

"Yes." The club manager was almost crying.

"That's what we are here for," Grijpstra said. "We are investigating whether a golf ball can kill a human being. So a drive would do it." He pointed. "The baron was in the pavilion. You said you were over there—at what, a hundred yards' distance? Your ball would have had enough force, you think?"

Baldert nodded. "But it missed him. Maybe it was close, whizzed by the baron, so to speak. Maybe it missed him by just a few inches."

"So much for a drive," Grijpstra said. "How about another type of shot? Like up"—the adjutant pointed at a cloud—"then down."

"Like with a mortar," de Gier said. "A howitzer."

"You mean a chip," Baldert said, "or an approach shot."

Grijpstra nodded good-humoredly. "The names don't much matter."

"No velocity that way," Baldert said. "It would have to be a drive."

"And what kind of distance would you need for a

killing shot?" de Gier asked.

"Would *I* need?"

"Would *one* need," de Gier said, swinging an imaginary golf club himself.

Baldert was getting nervous again. "You just said it. Within a hundred yards maybe. But *I* was only taking a practice swing. I didn't know there was a ball on the ground. No idea how it got there."

They had reached Baldert's office. Baldert kept stretching out his hands towards de Gier, while he talked about the dead baron, who, he claimed, wasn't merely a financial backer. Baron Hilger van Hopper was Baldert Gudde's good friend. He showed them a large photograph, silver framed. The baron, an aristocratic figure in a gold-braided uniform, wearing a tell bearskin hat, was on a horse, held by young Baldert. Baldert was a hussar too, with a corporal's double chevron on the sleeve of his tunic.

Baldert displayed two more photographs, in a double silver frame, dominating another sideboard. The baron, now a cadaverous-looking old man, smiled down on a dark young man in a spotless white tuxedo. The young man smiled up at him. In the second photograph the scene was mirrored. The baron was the same, smiling the other way down now. The dark young man was different.

"These guys are princes?" Grijpstra asked.

Baldert guffawed.

"They are not princes?"

"Who knows?" Baldert asked. "It was a joke. The baron wanted a party."

"I wouldn't display photos of a man I tried to kill with a golf ball in my private office," Baldert said. "You can ask around. I'm a nice guy. Check my horoscope. Aquarius stands for brotherly love. I have some Capricorn aspects, too. Capricorns are loyal." He stretched his arms again, wiggled his fingers at de Gier. "But if you wish to arrest me, please go ahead." Baldert was making funny faces now, like a clown might, Grijpstra thought, even when he knows that his final and hopeless grimace will fail to lift the audience's indifference.

The detectives tried to forget Baldert's performance as they left the town of Crailo.

Grijpstra visualized mussel soup, simmering in the immediate future. De Gier composed images of a Chinese take-out meal before going to his Papuan concert. The motorway traffic headed to Amsterdam moved slowly, then came to a stop. Cars honked, and drivers got out and leaned against their vehicles. An all-terrain patrol car nosed along the emergency lane and stopped next to the detectives' Fiat. The Rijkspolitie constable at the wheel stared at de Gier, then motioned to him to lower the window.

De Gier complied. "What's up?"

"What's down?" the constable said. "An eighteen-wheeler tank truck is down. There is inflammable fluid over all six lanes of the motorway. This will take hours."

"Ah," de Gier said, planning to stick his magnetic blue revolving light to the top of their Fiat, use the siren and drive ahead on the emergency lane. "I see. Thank you."

"No," the uniformed state police constable said. "We're keeping the strip free for fire engines. You can drive back if you like. My lieutenant suggests dinner in Crailo. At the Green Herring restaurant. He'll meet you there." The constable saluted before driving off. His mate smiled widely and waved.

"This is an unmarked car," de Gier said to Grijpstra. "All our gear is hidden. Are we that obvious?"

"Never underestimate our pastoral colleagues," Grijpstra said. "Rural incest can achieve miraculous genetic results. Don't you know extrasensory perception is quite common in the country?"

Crailo is a town of few streets. The restaurant occupied a low building with wide eaves. Small gnarled trees spread their branches protectively in front of the restaurant's whitewashed walls. Flowering impatiens plants, growing from oak half-barrels on both sides of the open front door, made splashes of delicate colors.

The detectives played three-ball billiards for a while. De Gier kept scoring. Grijpstra thumped the fat end of his stick impatiently on the floor. "Go on, miss!"

"I would if I could," de Gier said before his ball went wide.

The Crailo-based Rijkspolitie lieutenant, a wide-shouldered giant wearing a blue blazer and gray slacks and a blue tie over a white shirt, presented himself. He showed his ID.

"How did your constable spot us?" de Gier asked.

"Aren't you in my territory?" the widely smiling lieutenant said. His rumbling voice and strong, perfect teeth impressed the detectives.

The lieutenant guided his guests to a round table in the rear of the room. He hovered over his guests.

"May I recommend the stewed eel," the lieutenant said as he sat down between his guests. "Your dinners are on me. French fries included. You pay for the beer.

"I caught the eel, you see," the lieutenant said as the dish was served. "I keep quite a few eel traps. I'm sorry to keep you from going home but because of that overturned truck…"

"That was true?" Grijpstra asked. "You're not just waylaying us?"

The lieutenant looked hurt.

"Maybe we should have told you ahead of time that we were going to see this golf gent, eh?" Grijpstra asked.

The lieutenant agreed. He talked for a while, after ordering Heineken Export. He frowned while he toasted them. He suggested that maybe city detectives should alert Rural Law Enforcement before meddling with a local suspect. He suggested that maybe city detectives, if they didn't want to attract notice, shouldn't drive a brand-new compact, of such a poisonous green color, that a Rijks-politie helicopter, checking traffic on the A1 motorway, could identify the car at once.

"Baldert contacted you?" de Gier asked, peering at the lieutenant across the foam of his beer.

"We had no idea Baldert was your suspect," Grijpstra said. "The Amsterdam chief-constable sometimes plays golf here. To us, Baldert is an expert. We were told to research whether, and how, a golf ball can kill. Our commander in chief recommended..."

The lieutenant wasn't pacified yet. He accused his guests of being secretive busybodies. Referring to higher authority could not be considered as an excuse. Besides, if the chief of the Amsterdam police didn't trust local judgment, he could tell local judgment that to its face. To send sneaky types in a bright green toy compact...

"I like this place," de Gier said, looking around him. "The low solid beams, the antique tool collection displayed on the walls, the history embodied in these ancient surroundings." He looked at the lieutenant. "You know I exist in a concrete apartment?"

"Why would Baldert inform you about our visit?" Grijpstra asked.

The lieutenant shrugged. "The asshole feels guilty. He was brought up with narrow values. This is still the Bible Belt here."

"But did Baldert actually kill the baron?"

"I think the baron killed himself," the lieutenant said.

"You know the definition of intelligence? Making optimal use of a given set of circumstances? Baron Hilger van Hopper went even further. He actually manipulated—" He looked at de Gier. "Do you know how difficult it is to manipulate circumstances?"

"Very tricky," de Gier admitted.

"Almost impossible," the lieutenant said. "Things happen. The best thing we can do is happen along as best we can. But the baron set up that perverted wedding." He moodily stirred his stewed eels.

"Did Baldert want to kill the baron?" Grijpstra asked.

The lieutenant nodded. "That's the whole thing. The baron holds a huge mortgage on Baldert's golf club. Baldert is late with two or three payments, the baron forecloses. We have a recession going on. The bank won't refinance."

"And the guy is gay," de Gier said. "Is that what you mean by the baron setting himself up? He intended to drive Baldert crazy with jealousy?" De Gier also stirred his stewed eel moodily. "This is getting complicated. A master-servant relationship. A gay relationship. And all of it twisted."

"How sick can we get?" Grijpstra asked.

"The baron wasn't feeling well," the lieutenant said.

"So you treated the case as a potential murder?"

The lieutenant mentioned availability of key ingredients: ample motivation, opportunity, Baldert's presenting himself all the time, getting in the way, saying it wasn't his fault, lying. He was taking practice shots. There was a ball there. No, there wasn't. Well maybe there was.

"Okay," Grijpstra said. "So champion Baldert aimed a murderous golf ball at his former master's head and missed and felt guilty, either about aiming or missing, or both, but why do you suppose that we knew anything about that? Had we known, we would have come to see you, but the chief-constable said…"

"We were set up too," de Gier said. "You see, our own chief, who is working on a case in New York, has us researching the concept of driving a golf ball as a means of effecting death. Neither the adjutant nor I play golf. The Amsterdam chief-constable is the only golfer we know. Maybe our own chief knew that. Maybe he also knew of our chief-constable's being concerned about this murder in Crailo. Maybe our chief planned this, steering us toward the chief-constable. Now the chief-constable directs us toward his own golf club, the Crailo Club, and sets us up to stumble into your case, to bring about a fresh approach. Maybe our own chief, chief of detectives, a sly old mouse, tried to kill two birds with one goddamn stone…"

"…with one goddamn golf ball," Grijpstra said, "and here you apprehend us, goofing around your Mister Bad Conscience…."

The lieutenant, drinking more beer, picked up on Bad Conscience. He was, somewhat incoherently, but staying within certain limits, talking about how bad guys get caught. Bad guys want to get caught and therefore deliberately trip themselves up, and all law enforcement has to do is pick the suckers up, handcuff the suspects, take them to trial. The only reason that law enforcement works is because of suspects tripping themselves. But Baldert had tripped himself up twice. Baldert's fate would therefore be the ultimate horror. No human punishment for the baron killer. Limbo forever. Baldert in purgatory.

De Gier reminded the lieutenant of basic police law. "We, the police, are required to do our utmost to restore the citizens' peace of mind. We are supposed to work toward mutual benefit. The law actually says so. We are supposed to take care of the needy: emotionally, physically, whatever is needed. If Baldert wants to regain his peace of mind by getting arrested you might…"

The lieutenant poured more beer.

Grijpstra, in between drinking more beer, saw a way out. There were the circumstances. Baldert kept providing incriminating evidence. Yes, suspect admitted to organizing the plastic wind-up duck race. Why? Because it would attract all the partying guests down to the pond. From there they couldn't see Baldert swinging his club. Yes, it was ridiculous for Baldert, the golf club's owner and manager, and the organizer of the so-called wedding party, to practice his drive at that moment. Yes, the hundred-yard distance between Baldert swinging his club and the baron lolling in his chair in the pavilion would enable the ball to arrive at killing speed. Yes, Baldert was gay. Yes, the baron was gay. Yes, the baron and Baldert went back a long way, to glorious army days. Yes, the baron was known to sit in the cane chair in the pavilion, drinking and smoking and sniffing, until he fell over. Yes, Baldert missed him on purpose, just by a few inches, to shock the baron into sudden death.

"If that isn't cold-blooded planning," Grijpstra said, "if that isn't premeditated first-class murder…"

The lieutenant, drinking more beer, doubted the underlying strength of his case. Baldert's championship shot had missed. He didn't know about missing. Didn't murder require hitting?

"Attempted murder?" Grijpstra pleaded.

The lieutenant wouldn't risk that. He hated being made a fool of in court.

"Poor Baldert," Grijpstra said.

De Gier shook his head. "The way that poor devil kept offering me his wrists for handcuffs."

Grijpstra wouldn't give up yet. "The autopsy didn't help? Would you tell us about that?"

The lieutenant wished for nothing more than a chance to share that experience. Somehow he hadn't gotten to see an autopsy until Baron Hilger van Hopper's emaciated corpse was stretched out on the morgue table in the nearby city of Bussum. He ordered more stewed eels. The waitress served, making a bit of a mess, because she looked the other way as she dug about the seemingly writhing bodies.

Grijpstra, who had phoned Nellie with a request to freeze his portion of the mussel soup, liked seafood. He didn't mind so much that the stewed eels seemed to be moving about in "their juice." That's what de Gier was saying. De Gier was fond of seafood too but the eels looked strange.

"Their juice," the lieutenant laughed. He sucked up a fat piece. "Delicious," the lieutenant said. "You know how come they grow so nicely in these parts? You'll never guess. It's because we have fur farms nearby. As there is no market for the fur-bearing animals' carcasses the waste product gets dumped into the sea around here. Eels thrive on carrion."

"The autopsy?" Grijpstra asked.

The lieutenant described how a small circular saw had cut into the baron's skull, and how long knives cut out the dead man's entrails.

De Gier gently pushed his plate away.

"The autopsy's result?" Grijpstra asked. "Any signs of severe bruising? Broken ribs?"

Not a sign, the lieutenant said. If there had been a ball whizzing by, and he personally believed there had been, it traveled clear through the open pavilion.

Grijpstra sighed. "So what did Baron Hilger van Hopper die of?"

The pathologist's verdict had been "depletion of all life systems due to total physical exhaustion, due again to overstimulation by a lethal combination of alcohol and other drugs."

"Opium up his ass," the lieutenant said. "There was that too. He used suppositories. Too vain to suffer needle marks. Can you imagine? And as for the contents of the baron's intestines—"

De Gier got up abruptly.

"Are you okay now?" Grijpstra asked, after de Gier had gotten back into the Fiat, some five miles out of Amsterdam, near a cluster of dwarf pines decorating the bank of the A1 motorway.

De Gier wasn't sure.

"It will be hard to find emergency lanes closer to the city," Grijpstra said. "Try those pines again. You'll have something to hold on to. It's hard to vomit out of a car's window."

A municipal police patrol car stopped. Grijpstra showed his identification. The constable sniffed. "Beer? How many?" Grijpstra told the constable about stewed eel, carrion and an autopsy related to a murder case he and the sergeant had been forced to imagine in progress. He went into details while de Gier vomited within hearing distance.

"Yech," the constable said.

"Our colleagues should be informed that they handle their vehicle too roughly," de Gier said, after watching the patrol car jump back into traffic. "I hope you noted a number."

De Gier had, while holding on to a tree, been thinking, about golf.

Grijpstra had been thinking too, about Central Park.

The detectives agreed that they had chased a red herring.

"Not fish," de Gier said.

"Goose," Grijpstra said, "wild goose. You think he really set us up to go to Crailo? Or could this be stupidity?"

De Gier still didn't feel well.

Grijpstra drove for a while. "You have been to New York."

De Gier had, twice. On both occasions he had walked through Central Park. It's what you did in New York. The park had impressed him. He had listened to jazz, rowed some ladies across a pond, watched caged wild animals, observed children on a carousel, dodged bicyclists and joggers. He was sure nobody would be allowed to play golf there. Golf would be too dangerous, like having people taking rifle practice. He had seen folks playing baseball and football on playing fields behind the Metropolitan Museum, so maybe Uncle Bert had been hit by a random ball that covered some immense distance. But why think of *golf*?

"Immense distance?" Grijpstra asked.

When de Gier interviewed Johan Termeer, the nephew, Jo had placed the death of his uncle near the Sheep Meadow. The Sheep Meadow, as de Gier recalled, was over a kilometer from the ball playing fields he remembered.

"You didn't tell me," Grijpstra said.

It hadn't occurred to de Gier to question the commissaris's line of thinking. It did now. De Gier liked that. "It's nice not being able to hold on to things, isn't it?"

"Bah," Grijpstra said. "Now then. If anyone in Central Park were playing golf, which you say no one would, they would hit their balls nearly a mile from where Termeer was found. So we are wasting our time. And the chief is wasting his."

Relying on the given situation and their knowledge of the commissaris's personality and capacity of endurance, Grijpstra and de Gier diagnosed temporarily impaired judgment due to stress, plus depression about his forth-coming retirement. The old man was ill. He had been limping and coughing when de Gier saw him off at Schiphol Airport. He would now be required to run about in strange territory while attending fatiguing lectures. Pursuing the Termeer case had to be an unbearable extra burden.

"He needs help," Grijpstra said.

Chapter 8

The commissaris had planned to see, and to interrogate if possible, the mounted female officer whose horse had been in contact with the older Termeer, and to pay a visit to Termeer's neighbor Charlie, but the codeine had worn him out and he had trouble getting up. His dreams had been bothersome again. He dragged himself to Le Chat Complet where Mamère served him coffee instead of the tea he ordered, saying, "You mess too much with tea, monsieur." She brought him crisp croissants and fresh strawberry jam. He was told to have patience regarding the boiled eggs he had ordered.

While eating his breakfast he reflected on his nightly adventures. His dreams the previous night seemed more complicated than before. Once again the tram driver played the leading part. The commissaris was a little boy, on his way to school. He wore short pants and a jacket that were hand-me-downs from his older brother, Therus. The boy-commissaris was carrying his lunch in a foldable metal lunchbox, closed with a red band of elastic. The tram driver wanted to share his lunch, after asking him, via the tram's intercom, to come over and sit next to her. "Little boy in the hand-me-down clothing, come and sit up here with me," hidden speakers in the car said. It was embarrassing. It also made him jealous. He didn't want to share the tram driver's wonderful presence with his fellow passengers.

The commissaris remembered that, in the dream, the tram driver's voice was deep and husky. He wondered what this could mean. Was he feeding a demon or a goddess? The sharing of his cheese sandwiches and apple with the long-legged creature had been erotically interesting, despite the fact — or maybe because — his dream companion stared at him with empty eye sockets. The commissaris remembered that, as a young boy, adult women, when they displayed their legs, often drove him mad with desire.

What could the symbol of the blond tram driver's legs have to do with his present quest?

Cats were passing the restaurant's windows and the three musicians behind the counter were harmonizing their song, much encouraged by the café's clients.

The commissaris concentrated on the painting of the youthful and naked Mamère and her tongue-lolling dog under the palm tree of her native Haiti.

"You like?" the real Mamère asked when she finally served the eggs. He nodded. She pointed at the huge painting. "That was dreamtime when I got my sons." She named the men behind the café's counter. "Dieudonné, Zazeu and FilsTrois," Mamère said proudly. "I very fertile then."

"Beautiful voices Dieudonné, Zazeu and FilsTrois have," the commissaris said.

"You better accent in French than in English," Mamère said. "What you do for profession?"

The commissaris said that he was a policeman from Amsterdam, investigating the recent death of a country-man, another *Hollandais*, near Central Park West.

"Ah," Mamère said noncommittally, then rushed off to pour more coffee.

Back in his suite the commissaris still had a few minutes before he was to be picked up. He looked down at the park. There were benches there where people kept sitting down and getting up. Young men on roller skates whizzed around at high speed. The commissaris noticed a system in the complicated movements, a well-organized activity. He concluded that, possibly, drugs were being dealt. He watched a young woman, dressed in a neat suit with a tailored blouse: an office worker, a secretary maybe. She made signs at one of the roller skaters. She raised her left hand, made a fist, then made her thumb pop up. Then she got up and sat down on another bench. The roller skater sped by the vacated bench and scooped up a green piece of paper. Another roller skater passed the waiting woman and dropped something in her lap.

There was a knock at the door. Chief O'Neill came in. "How're you doing, Yan?"

Yan was doing fine. He showed O'Neill what was going on below.

O'Neill nodded. "The roller skaters are members of Trevor's gang. Small stuff. Dime bags. Retail bullshit. We're after Trevor for the murder of Maggotmaid. Or, rather, Hurrell is after Trevor." The chief smiled. "We all have our hang-ups."

O'Neill talked about Trevor while he drove the commissaris to the lecture. Traffic was congested, but they had ample time. The commissaris learned why Hurrell was particularly interested in Trevor E. Lee, an oil heir from Houston who had wasted his fortune and was now going all out to make up for his losses.

"It's kind of personal," O'Neill said. "Hurrell has just got to get Trevor. I don't like that much but I think we better give in a bit, for the sergeant's peace of mind." O'Neill grinned. "If there is such a thing. A contradiction in terms. How can something as essentially restless as a mind be peaceful?"

"Just before falling asleep," the commissaris said.

O'Neill laughed. "Or when it isn't working." He tapped the commissaris's arm. "Here is the deal with Trevor. Trevor killed Maggotmaid, we're sure of that. He got her up for the party, plied her with heroin, got her on a table for a sex show and discovered she was male. Or had been male. She'd had the operation. Russo didn't mention *that* at the lecture."

"Oh dear," the commissaris said. "And you can't arrest the suspect?"

"Not with the kind of prosecutors I have to deal with," O'Neill said. He looked grim as he raced the car to beat traffic lights. "And not with the kinds of mistakes our detectives are making. Tom and Jerry—again—somehow managed to mess up the glass. The glass on Maggotmaid's clothes and the glass in the broken door in Trevor's apartment matched, but the evidence got mixed up. You ever have shit like that happen?"

"Oh yes," the commissaris said, "but we're short of cells, so arrests aren't welcome."

O'Neill frowned furiously. "We have the same problems. Quality-of-life offenses? Pickpocketing? Forget it. Overcrowded jails, overcrowded dockets. So Trevor walks. But Hurrell will find a way to kick him into the slammer sometime soon."

The commissaris muttered as the big Chevrolet hurled itself between two buses.

"How?" O'Neill asked, touching his horn playfully. "It's more like why. You see, Hurrell's only child went bad. Young Henry Hurrell became Henriette. But there was no operation. The parents weren't too thrilled and I guess they made the kid miserable. So did the other kids. A nail that sticks out gets hammered sometimes. So

Henriette comforted herself with drugs. Mrs. Hurrell left the scene. She divorced Earl and the custody of the youngster went to the father. Mother transferred to a quiet sunny town in Arizona where everybody is so old that the worst they can do is sue each other. The former Mrs. Hurrell couldn't cope with a fourteen-year-old prostituting herself for heroin."

"Himself," the commissaris said.

"Nah." O'Neill shook his head. "I sort of knew the kid, ran into her a few times, and she was definitely female, never mind what her sexual organs looked like. She had a female personality, soft and gentle, but that must have changed because she looked like a scarecrow when they found her with the garbage."

"Garbage," the commissaris said. "Right. Sergeant Hurrell seemed bitter about 'garbage.' 'Human garbage,' he said."

"A cold night." O'Neill shook a friendly fist at a yellow taxi closing in, trying to cut him off, but not quite managing it. "Bet you that cabbie is from Ghana. Probably had his driver's license printed up special." He shook his head. "You know, we laugh at those guys, and curse them, but can you imagine what it is like to get thrown into this city and nothing makes sense and you're supposed to drive a goddamn *taxi*?"

"A cold night," the commissaris said. "You were talking about Hurrell's transvestite child."

"Right. Human garbage. The kid doesn't go home

anymore, is living on the street. Hustles like crazy to keep the opium monkey fed. Picks up the disease from a dirty needle, gets pneumonia. God knows what assortment of deadly diseases those junkie whores collect during the course of one day." O'Neill looked sideways at the commissaris. "But the body persists. Think of the German death camps—bodies lived through that for quite a while sometimes. Abuse, starvation, it looks like we humans like to suffer. One early winter morning the kid faints. Next thing she freezes solid. We don't have too many real cold nights in New York but we do have a few killers. Gets rid of a lot of the homeless." O'Neill raised his voice. "Goddamn homeless, I hate them. You know why? They scare me shitless. Here we are, the most powerful country on the globe and we have human wrecks messing up our recreation areas, crapping around statues, pissing up public transport, dragging their sodden bodies about everywhere. If we can't cure their insane uselessness why don't we just warehouse those wrecks in some nice warm camp some-where, with lots of TV and junk food and innocuous games to play? But no, sir, we need more aircraft carriers, for we've got to bomb holes in brown people's countries."

"I like America," the commissaris said.

O'Neill grumbled. "So do I. This is the place. I want to drive cross-country again, or hang out in the Keys. I used to work summers there, crew on sailboats. Or go to Hawaii again, hard to be unhappy in Hawaii, right? They've got it all there." He gestured. "We've got it all everywhere, and if it ain't, UPS will deliver it tomorrow morning. Coast to coast. And anywhere in between."

"And the UPS driver will speak English," the commissaris said. "And the currency will be dollars."

"Efficiency, right?" O'Neill laughed. "I've been to Europe and you have to change language every two hours, but you can't, so you're in trouble. And the backdrops seem so small there." He gestured toward the World Trade Center's twin towers. "Big stuff here." He raised an eyebrow at the commissaris. "You've traveled around in this country?"

The commissaris had been to Maine once. He talked about coves, bays, hills that looked like mountains to a Dutchman. "Few people around. Amazing wildlife. Holland now imports its wildlife from Poland and then has to buy more because it starves or gets poached. Ravens, wild boars, deer—it's hard to share a square mile with nine hundred Dutchmen."

"Lots of lobsters in Maine." O'Neill was frowning again. "But you freeze your ass off in winter." He touched the commissaris's bare wrist. "Know what some jokers did with frozen Henriette? Stuck her in a fifty-five-gallon trash can, upside down. You've seen the signs? DON'T LITTER."

The commissaris had seen the signs.

"Those jokers tried to burn the corpse too, but they ran out of lighter fuel."

The commissaris mumbled disapproval.

"Hurrell caught them," O'Neill said. "A neat piece of detection. Lot of work. This happened early in the morning, when there are only bakers around, paperboys, cheap whores, maybe some sleepless old person looking out of a window."

"He found witnesses like that?" The commissaris sounded surprised.

O'Neill nodded. "Sure did. Hurrell's name isn't in the report because he couldn't take the credit. The defense would claim that he, as the kid's father, was biased."

"Suspects convicted?"

"Yeah," O'Neill said. "The D.A. charged the jokers with intentional and unlawful mutilation of a corpse. That's a felony. One to three years in the clinker."

"And now Sergeant Hurrell won't pay attention to the death of Bert Termeer," the commissaris said, "because he sees Maggotmaid as Henriette, his own child."

"He'll get Trevor," O'Neill said. "You saw what is going on in Central Park, right under your window. Central Park is Hurrell's turf. He'll work the park, get the right statements and hit Trevor with a heavy drug charge."

The commissaris could think of other charges. He tried to translate them from the Netherlandic Penal Code. "Attempted manslaughter — Trevor pushed Maggotmaid through a glass door, causing death by negligence twice, first by administering an overdose of a controlled substance, second by locking, and leaving, a body in the hot and unventilated trunk of a parked car."

O'Neill concentrated on his driving.

"What do you think, Chief?"

O'Neill growled. "None of that will stick." He sighed. "Hurrell is using the right tactics. He pretends he's finished with Trevor, lulling him to sleep, so to speak. He wants to catch Trevor carrying at least a kilo."

O'Neill parked the car. They got out and began to walk. "But you have no case anyway. Bert Termeer died of disease, and maybe exposure." He grinned at the commissaris. "There is no doubt in my mind that the Termeer death was from natural causes. I want to close the case."

The commissaris agreed. He had studied the reports the previous night, seen the photographs. Now he had an expert opinion as formulated by an experienced colleague. The commissaris was about to tell Chief O'Neill that he agreed that Termeer's death was due to an unfortunate combination of circumstances beyond the control of any human agency.

It was just a coincidence, he told himself, that a touring bus appeared. The bus displayed a big number 2 up front. The driver was a blond young woman with heavily made-up eyes. She stopped her huge vehicle soundlessly so that the little old gentleman, walking with some difficulty and the help of a gold-tipped cane, could cross the street at his ease. The commissaris raised his cane in thanks.

The driver waved.

"Strange-looking woman," O'Neill said, walking next to the commissaris. "Macabre makeup. Did you see those eyes?"

Chapter 9

Amsterdam's chief-constable wasn't ready to sign the document that Grijpstra had brought along and placed on his superior's desk. The CC was talking about playing golf at Crailo and the sudden death of his friend the baron.

Grijpstra's comments had been conversational. "Beautiful course, sir," and "Yes, that was unfortunate, wasn't it?"

The chief-constable smiled.

Grijpstra felt encouraged. He moved the request for funding further across the desk. "Could you please sign this, sir?"

The CC looked away.

Grijpstra sighed. "You are concerned about the possibility of foul play, sir?"

The chief-constable talked at some length. He said that, in spite of what he was doing at his present elevated position, which, as most insiders were aware of, was mostly decorative these days, he was still a cop at heart and therefore curious about human erring. A man had died at the Crailo Golf Club of which the CC was an active member.

Grijpstra's rugged face plied itself into an expression of interest. "You and the baron were friends, sir?"

Friends...friends...the chief-constable said he didn't known about "friends." "Friends are like clouds in the sky, Adjutant. They float around, they disappear, they come back in different shapes, you reach out and they're gone again."

Grijpstra said he liked clouds himself. He often tried to paint them.

"Really?" the CC asked. "I thought you mostly portrayed dead ducks."

"With clouds above them," Grijpstra said. "For contrast, maybe. The dead ducks are upside down in the canals, with bright orange feet which make them sail along." The adjutant's gestures showed how this was done. "And the white clouds bring out the bright orange."

The chief-constable smiled again. He hadn't listened. He was talking in a barely audible voice when he admitted to a personal interest in what he referred to as the "Crailo murder." He had known Hilger van Hopper fairly well, had been following the ups and downs of the baron's life at close quarters. "But it seemed the poor fellow was going mostly down, Adjutant. Which amazed me." The chief-constable spoke with more enthusiasm now. "Hilger was a smart fellow, educated, insightful, one might say. A cynic. You know what a cynic is, Adjutant?"

Grijpstra thought a cynic was one who mocked generally accepted human values.

The CC explained that there was no mockery here, but a sincere disbelief, based on observation. A cynic, he said, has found reasons to believe that all human activity is based on selfishness. "Do you believe that, Adjutant?" The CC's smile was sad. "I rather do so myself."

Grijpstra nodded convincingly while he pushed his documents a little further across the vast emptiness of the desk between them.

"Yes," the chief-constable said. "Hilger, therefore, was out for himself. In a pleasant way. He was a baron, of course."

"A nobleman," Grijpstra said pleasantly. "Noble."

"Noble selfishness," the CC said. He held his long elegant hands back above the polished top of his desk. His fingertips played the scherzo of Chopin's *Klaviersonate Nr. 2 b-moll op. 35*. Grijpstra knew the sonata because he had been made to play it himself, as a boy, after his teachers determined that he had musical talent. Grijpstra had wanted to try Billy Strayhorn compositions. He still did.

"So," the CC said, "here we have a superior sort of chap who has figured out that we are in it for ourselves, and who has the means to indulge himself, and who is all out to make one good time flow into another."

Grijpstra looked surprised. "He did not succeed?"

The CC shook his head. He tried to share a congenial grin with Grijpstra. "No, he just kept losing. But then he was suddenly in the money again, with a loving wife and a handsome lover, and then he managed to suddenly lose his life."

Grijpstra contemplated his ultimate chief's appearance. Amsterdam's police commander in chief was a decorative man: tall, slim, silver haired, with an aquiline nose. He was reputed to suffer from depression. After his wife died, crashing her airplane into a peat bog, the CC engaged in brief relationships, often with women he knew through his work. The grapevine reported that they all had the same comment: that the CC wasn't part of the activities he engaged in. Although he performed the correct movements, his behavior was mechanical, all while being polite and charming. The CC took his lovers out to plays and concerts, and paid for good dinners. He listened, laughed at jokes and tipped the waiters. "But he is mostly dead," the women reported.

Grijpstra wondered whether he could interact with a man who was mostly dead.

"Baldert's projectile, the golf ball, did miss the baron."

"Maybe that was just part of what caused my friend's loss of life," the CC said. "What if Baldert, after narrowly missing his easy target, and after noticing that the baron was experiencing some sort of attack, stroke or what have you, had called an ambulance?"

"According to the rural lieutenant," Grijpstra said, "it seems your golf companion was dangling from the last strand of the end of his tether."

"A stretched metaphor." The CC laughed. "The commissaris is right, you *are* a card."

Grijpstra apologized. "Wasn't meaning to be funny, sir."

The chief-constable leaned back in his executive's revolving chair. His voice was sad. "Causing death by omission of some activity, an interesting construction, Adjutant. I wrote my thesis on that."

Grijpstra moved the document another millimeter. "Sir?"

The CC's fingers now played the sonata's next movement, the "Marche funèbre." To be played, Grijpstra remembered, *"lento-attacca."*

"Missed on purpose?" Grijpstra asked. "But the ball passed close by the victim's head. The baron now realizes that Baldert, whom he considered to be his friend, is trying to kill him. The shock sets off a heart attack. And then Baldert, still as part of the plan, pretends to panic and doesn't call an ambulance until the crowd returns from watching plastic windup ducks?"

The CC's fingertips were moving.

The chief was talking almost inaudibly again: "...my wife would still be alive if I had made sure that the old Cessna had been properly checked. I knew that the mechanics at the Air Club were sloppy. But I didn't like her, you see."

Grijpstra stared.

"I didn't like my wife," the chief-constable said. He smiled. He stopped playing the sonata, pulled the form toward him and signed it with a flourish. "There you are," the CC said pleasantly. "This will pay for de Gier's airfare and expenses. I am glad that you fellows are concerned about the commissaris's welfare." He looked up. "So how is the old man doing?"

Grijpstra thought that the commissaris was ill.

"He has been ill for years now," the CC said. "He could have been on permanent sick leave since he started using a cane." He looked at his long slender hands, then dropped them under the desk top. "But maybe my respected colleague doesn't like doing nothing."

"What are *you* going to do, sir?" Grijpstra asked. "When you retire?"

The chief-constable smiled. "I will just fade away, Adjutant. I am good at that. I have been practicing for years."

Grijpstra, as he left the room, remembered the commissaris saying that lack of substance makes people float to the top.

"Yessir," the adjutant said. "Thank you." He waved his signed document. "This will get things going."

Chapter 10

Detective-Sergeant de Gier, six thousand miles west of his jurisdiction, helicoptered from Kennedy Airport to the Heliport on Manhattan's East Side.

New York impressed him. The spectacular city looked the part of a major power center. Manhattan's unique skyline convinced de Gier that whatever was thought up here would cause ripples all around the planet, for a while anyway. Nothing is forever but what force could wipe out this metropolis of glass and steel? Warfare? Internal strife? One of the modern drug-resistant plagues? He wondered if someday an earthquake would topple those splendid tall buildings.

Would some people be crushed by their own top-heavy creations and the rest flee? He knew about the abandoned cities of Central and South America, where the jungle had reclaimed huge buildings. Not only did the citizens disappear, but there was no memory of what might have happened. Yet there was obviously technology there, knowledge, a high degree of organization, a well-developed infrastructure. Anthropologists had come up with vague theories, in which facts didn't fit.

Would the New York skyscrapers degenerate into crumpled shapes leaning across each other, with skeletons staring out of broken windows? Would vines, mold, lichens and mosses gradually smooth their jumbled lines?

Maybe, de Gier thought, it will all slide into the ocean, to the bottom of the sea, like Atlantis, like Amsterdam. With Amsterdam there is the certainty, in a foreseeable, calculable future, that the sea will flood the city. Ice caps melt and ocean levels rise and dikes cannot be built up forever.

There would be fish again, huge schools, unbothered by hunger at the top of the food chain. De Gier imagined fish swimming through his apartment.

"Quite a place you have here," de Gier told the Trump Air stewardess. He read her the address of a bed and breakfast Antoinette had written down in his notebook. Antoinette and Karel had enjoyed the place. How to get there?

"Horatio Street?" the stewardess asked. De Gier had his map out. She pointed the way. "A little bit complicated. The subway is cheap but I would advise a cab."

He found coordinates for the Cavendish on his map

and thought that he might contact the commissaris first. There was plenty of time. It wouldn't do to make things easy. If New York was to be his hunting ground for the next few days he should investigate on foot. A cab was too easy. He told the stewardess he would call on a friend first, proudly reciting the address: Eighty-third and Fifth.

He only carried a leather shoulder bag holding three changes of linen, a CD player, six Miles Davis CDs and a novel by Alvaro Mutis, in the original Spanish. De Gier had been puzzling through the tale during the flight across the Atlantic. His Spanish was poor and he hadn't brought a dictionary, so many words had to be guessed at. De Gier, a self-taught linguist, had managed to wade halfway through the first chapter. He had figured out what seemed to be a plot line. A writer of technical brochures on petrochemical subjects travels to Finland. It's cold in Helsinki. The protagonist goes to the harbor from where he can see the domes of St. Petersburg and watches a tramp steamer enter port. But now, to de Gier's delight, he is no longer in forty-degrees-below Finland but in ninety-degrees-above Honduras, where a woman in a bikini runs toward a yacht. In spite of her large feet she is attractive, due to good makeup. Her husband is shooting at seabirds with a .45 automatic, but misses.

"You're Spanish?" the stewardess asked, seeing the book in de Gier's hand. "You don't sound Spanish." She was smiling. The stewardess, like de Gier, was in her forties. De Gier had noticed that older women were now sending signals. De Gier, known at Amsterdam Headquarters as "Mr. B Movie," was tall, wide shouldered, athletic looking. Women liked his thick curly hair and huge cavalry-officer-style swept-up mustache. In potential sexual encounters he had been backing off lately, preferring the company of his cat. He had told Grijpstra, when the adjutant was about to be taken over by the hotel owner and former prostitute Nellie, "Animals have smaller brains but they use them better."

"You dislike women now?"

De Gier gestured all-inclusively. "I dislike people."

"You're people yourself."

"Anyone," de Gier said. But he didn't see himself so much. Only in the mirror.

"But you often look in mirrors," Grijpstra said. "You're very vain, you know. Combing your hair. Brushing up the old mustache."

De Gier didn't like vain people either.

The stewardess watched her passenger stride off, going west on Sixty-third Street. She liked the cut of his long linen breeches. The leather flight jacket looked good too. The fellow was probably gay, due to meet a clone on Horatio Street. The stewardess wished the pair luck as she picked up Dixie cups in the helicopter's cabin.

It was a nice day. De Gier walked, map in hand, up Fifth Avenue, glancing at Central Park, the grisly scene of Uncle Bert Termeer's demise, but the park looked pleasant. He reached the Cavendish and happened to meet the commissaris in the lobby.

"What?" the commissaris asked. "Is it *you?"*

De Gier said he had always wanted to visit New York again, that his last visit had been too short, that he had taken a few days off. And as he knew the commissaris was in town too he had thought he might look him up.

"How are you, sir?"

"That last time you were trailing me too," the commissaris said. He took off his round spectacles and furiously blew on the glasses. "Who is paying for this nonsense?"

"Yessir," de Gier said. "Nice day. I walked here from the river. I came in by chopper. Did you use the helicopter too? Beautiful, all those buildings. I have been reading this novel, sir, by a Colombian author, in Spanish. Do you have any idea what *'huevones'* means? I didn't bring a dictionary, you see. It's more fun to guess but sometimes I get lost a bit. The meaning of *huevones* escapes me."

The bellhop was a Latino who looked like a dwarfed Anthony Quinn. Thinking de Gier was a guest, he had come over to carry luggage. *"Huevones,"* the bellhop said, "literally means 'balls,' but what is the context, sir? Could you show me the passage?"

De Gier opened his book and found the relevant sentence. *"Si me llegan a dejar se mueren de hambre, huevones."*

"And the context?" the bellhop asked.

De Gier had figured out that a bikini-clad woman

was yelling at men on a boat, sailors who were about to take off without her, and that she wanted to go along, for she was the cook. She was yelling at the men that without her they would die of hunger.

"Ah," the bellhop said. "Then *'huevones'* should be taken as 'assholes,' as a derogatory term, sir. Where did you put your luggage?"

"You're not staying here," the commissaris told de Gier.

"I'm not staying here," de Gier told the bellhop.

"Jack of all trades," the bellhop said, pointing at his chest. "Teach Spanish, offer referrals for analysis of dreams." He handed over cards to the commissaris and de Gier. "Ignacio is the name, *a sus ordenes, señores*. Journeys can be arranged. Voodoo is an expensive option."

"Journeys?" de Gier asked.

"A Native American shortcut," the bellhop explained, "to the realm of collective subconscious spirits. We Mexicans are part Indian. But it may be that voodoo will explain your dreams better. My favorite black voodoo lady can guide you through all the netherworlds."

Netherlandic de Gier wanted to be clever. "I've just come from there."

Ignacio saluted. The reception clerk had rung her bell. The bellhop turned and ran.

"My golf blunder," the commissaris told de Gier while they ate in a nearby sushi restaurant, "alarmed you."

He peered at the sergeant. "Katrien thinks I am ill and you and Grijpstra think I am silly." His chopstick pointed between his eyes. "Daft in the head. I now need an attendant."

The chopstick pointed at de Gier's forehead. "Do you know that I attended a hit and run lecture this afternoon and that I couldn't concentrate on skid marks?"

"Well now…," de Gier soothed.

The commissaris spat urchin meat into his napkin. "You like raw fish, Rinus? Yes? That's good." He pushed his plate away. "Could be I'm stressed out. Or depressed maybe. Last puzzle of my career and I feel obliged to solve it. But so far it's all nonsense, and I have this damned flu, and there are all these lectures. Trying to pay attention. For what? *You* tell me." The commissaris's faded blue eyes stared through de Gier's head. "Improve my knowledge when I'm just about out?"

De Gier smiled. "Oh, but you will be with the police academy soon, and at Interpol and whatnot," de Gier said. "Policemen everywhere will benefit from your teaching."

"On deadly golf balls," the commissaris said. "Well, I know that much now. No golf in Central Park."

"You've seen the NYPD, sir?"

The commissaris, in between sneezing and coughing, reported on his conversations with Chief O'Neill and Detective-Sergeant Hurrell.

"A noncase," the commissaris concluded, "about to be closed. You type up a report and fax it home. Grijpstra, in due course, informs complainant that Uncle just fell over. Such things happen. Can't be helped." The commissaris felt his throat. "There is folded sandpaper in here,

Rinus. It grinds together when I swallow." His next sneeze made his spectacles fall off. De Gier caught them.

"Thank you, Sergeant. Case about to be closed. Even so…," the commissaris shivered, "…I feel we might look further. Try to do a good job. Just for the record. Or for no reason at all. For the hell of it, Sergeant. See the mounted policewoman. Call on Bert Termeer's landlord and neighbor, Charlie. Maybe we will do that tomorrow."

"You don't have a lecture tomorrow, sir?"

The commissaris checked his program. "On trace evidence, in the afternoon." He put the paper away. "Reminds me of the Maggotmaid case, which you should know about, Sergeant. Let me tell you why."

De Gier ate his raw octopus and boiled rice rolls while the commissaris related the story, featuring Detective-Sergeant Hurrell, as told by Chief O'Neill.

"Crawling maggots, eh?" de Gier asked.

The commissaris's teeth chattered.

"I'll take you to the hotel, sir."

The commissaris grimaced courageously. "An early night, a hot bath, try again tomorrow, Sergeant."

"Tomorrow and tomorrow and tomorrow," bellhop Ignacio said. "I thought millionaires like you guys wouldn't use that expression. I thought it was just us. I thought it was because of tomorrowism that guys like us will be hundredaires forever."

Ignacio, out of the Cavendish Hotel uniform, wearing a black silk suit, an open white shirt and high-heeled boots, seemed a different being.

The commissaris tried to smile between coughs. "Ignacio? From the hotel?"

"Happened to see you sitting here at the window," Ignacio said. "I often stop in here. I know one of the cooks. He gives me discount dinners."

"Care to join us?" the commissaris asked approvingly.

Ignacio declined with thanks. He pointed at the sushi. "Don't care for the Cavendish nouvelle cuisine undefinables, do you? Grind up and color, serve with a leaf of purple cabbage at fifty bucks a plate."

"It's all right," the commissaris said.

"Our breakfast is all right," Ignacio said, "but you like to eat that out too, don't you? With Mamère, the naked doggie lady?"

The commissaris looked surprised. "How do you know?"

"Bellhops," Ignacio said solemnly, "know everything."

"There is always an explanation," de Gier said.

"For the thinker and the seer." Ignacio looked at the commissaris. "Le Chat Complet is across the street. I saw you there yesterday. I know Mamère. After you left, Mamère said you'd had bad dreams lately. That's why I gave you the voodoo spiel earlier. She thinks you should see her."

The bell hop wished them a pleasant evening, then walked to the sushi bar to talk to the cook.

Chapter 11

De Gier, using the subway map Antoinette had lent him, figured out a quick way to get to Bleecker Street. After the ride he walked down Christopher and up Hudson and got to his bed and breakfast on Horatio by 8:00 P.M. After the loud bars and New Age display windows of the neighborhood's main streets Horatio looked neat. There were trees, the quaint houses were in excellent repair, cool fresh air wafted down from the Hudson River. The house he wanted had an imposing front door of varnished oak, decorated with a brass knocker. The establishment's owner, a small balding man in his fifties who introduced himself as Freddie, was happy to show his guest a well-equipped and tastefully furnished apartment. The bedroom viewed treetops. Freddie and his live-in friend, Antonio, a hospital nurse, a heavyset man with a big black beard, remembered Antoinette and her husband, Karel.

"Lovely couple," Freddie said. "I showed Karel around some of the galleries in SoHo. Admirable fellow, a spastic stutterer and yet in such good command of himself. Good artist. Showed me photos of his sculptures. So Karel and his wife recommended you? That's nice. And you are a policeman? You're here on business? Antoinette telephoned. She told us to be of use. Care to tell us about your mission?"

Antonio was enthusiastic too. He liked to read true crime stories and occasionally indulged in mystery fiction.

"We both like puzzles," Freddie said. "You have pieces we can fit together?"

The drinks, served on the tiny lawn, between hedges of wild roses, were all juices. Freddie and Antonio admitted to being recovering alcoholics.

"You mind?" Freddie asked.

De Gier said he had been thinking of cutting his own habit.

"Cutting down?"

"Cutting out."

"The only way," Antonio said. "And your case?"

De Gier explained.

Antonio was interested. He knew Central Park well. He sailed his model sailboat on the Model Boat Pond, kept it there in Kerb's Model Boat House. Being around Central Park on weekends he had seen most of what he called 'the crazies.' "An exhibitionist, you say? Could you let us have some details?"

De Gier provided the details he remembered from Reserve Constable Jo Termeer's description and the Lakmakers' report.

"I think I know the guy," Antonio said. "He stopped me once. Very nicely. Told me to 'watch it.'"

"Watch what?"

Antonio shrugged. "Just 'it,' I guess. To be aware, you know? To pay attention?"

"Like in the Boy Scouts," Freddie said. "Awareness is the key. Lord Baden Powell thought of that. Noble-looking old codger. What ever happened to the Boy Scouts?"

"Watch the bullshit going on," Antonio said. "I think your guy was telling me to watch all the bullshit."

"Like your own?" Freddie asked, winking at de Gier.

"Right." Antonio, ignoring Freddie's wink, nodded pleasantly. "Watch my own bullshit. Might save me some trouble. Think for myself."

De Gier, after restating his facts briefly again, proffered a theory that might interest his hosts. The theory aimed at explaining why Termeer might have been murdered. De Gier's hypothesis proposed that there were sexual overtones here. Even though Chief O'Neill claimed Termeer wasn't into nudity the man was obviously a performer. Also possibly demented. Standing still for hours, in some contorted attitude, and then dashing off, frolicking."

Freddie and Antonio laughed. "Like Snoopy... Snoopy likes to frolic in parks."

Right, de Gier said, but there could be more to the need to frolic. There were many cases in Amsterdam's Vondel Park where women danced around and, once they had attracted an audience, slipped out of their fur coats or cloaks and pranced about naked, and there were men who pretended to amuse little girls, by means of games or dolls, and then suddenly exposed themselves.

"So what do you cops do?" Antonio asked.

Nothing much, de Gier said. Take the foolish folks home maybe. Be kind and forgiving. Keep tensions down. Amsterdam is known for permissiveness, the city welcomes alternative lifestyles, but the American East Coast is known for more Puritan values. De Gier became enthusiastic. Now what if old Termeer had dared to point his pecker at a female cop, a mounted female cop, a dominatrix on a high horse? Wouldn't that get him in trouble? Get him kicked in the chest by the officer's horse? The perpetrator gallops off. Doesn't tell anyone what happened. Victim dies in the bushes. The NYPD covers up. Perhaps there was repressed anger in the policewoman's subconscious. Maybe she was of Puritan stock?

De Gier got up and walked excitedly around the small Horatio Street garden, acting out the scene. Imagine this extreme case of a supposedly neat old gent, in tweeds, with a lovely white beard, a St. Nick figure, dropping his mask by opening his fly, being utterly disgusting, provoking an impeccably uniformed law enforcement officer *by waving his dick at the goddamn woman?*

De Gier's audience was amused but not impressed. "No Puritans in New York," Freddie said.

Antonio agreed. "You're thinking of Massachusetts. Massachusetts was settled by hypocrites in hats. You guys, the Dutch, settled Manhattan. Flamboyant folks. 'New Amsterdam,' remember? And then, after you guys, it was the British. The Brits were merchants and aristocrats. They're not after dicks, they're after money." He laughed. "Money buys the good life, eh, Fred?"

Freddie told de Gier that he specialized in trading furniture and art objects from those early days. Through his dealings he had absorbed some of the distinctive atmosphere of that historical period. Neither the Dutch not the British had been concerned about prescribing restrictive behavior in order to impress a forbidding Father.

"Show him that picture of the cross-dressing governor, Freddie."

Freddie knew of a portrait of one of the Tory governors, a well-known transvestite. He went inside and came back with an art book. There was a full-page reproduction of an oil painting showing a powerful figure in an extravagant satin dress. "Here," Freddie said. "Mark the shaven jowls. His ladyship. An early J. Edgar Hoover."

"And the governor held court *here*," Antonio said, "in New York City. Nobody minded much."

De Gier's theory crumbled while Freddie and Antonio, taking turns, being careful not to interrupt each other, like TV anchormen, lectured him on the history of New York City. The sergeant was told that the city had been on the British side during the American Revolution and had spent the Civil War sympathizing with the southern slavery states.

"Bah!" Freddie concluded.

"Sin and corruption," Antonio said. "We have a bad name here; the rest of the country hates us. We like that. You think you guys are way-out in Holland? Go to Central Park, watch out-of-state wannabe-shockers try to be naughty in spandex shorts, in bare-bottom thongs, even…" Antonio grinned. "There was a bare-top guy on the Promontory in a kind of lampshade that he wore as a skirt. The shade folded up if he pulled a string, and then he'd pull another string and erect something that could be a Day-Glo-velvet-upholstered cucumber and waggle *that*"—Antonio looked at de Gier triumphantly—"and *still* nobody looked."

Freddie smiled. "We all know what Amsterdam is like today, but New York has long been there."

"More apricot juice?" Antonio asked.

"Some hazelnut latte with fat-free topping?" Freddie asked.

De Gier had both.

"Sorry to disappoint you," Antonio said. "But you've got to get real."

"You can't shock a New York policewoman," Freddie said. "That's Real for you." He cleared his throat.

"Eh, Rainus? That how you pronounce your name? Just one question. I should have asked you before. We don't tolerate smoking in this building. You don't use nicotine, do you? If you do we can easily find you other lodging."

De Gier claimed to have given up smoking some months before.

"And you didn't gain weight?" Antonio asked, looking down at his own protruding belly. "I gained forty pounds. It's two years now and I still haven't lost it."

"What's your secret, pal?" Freddie asked.

De Gier said he mostly ate sliced radishes on toast for breakfast and was spending more time on unarmed combat police training and repeated a mantra whenever he tended to think about chocolate.

"What mantra?"

De Gier blushed. "Nothing special."

"No slips?"

"Some slips."

"Doesn't that prolong the agony?"

"It does."

"How do you cope with agony?"

De Gier demonstrated. He got up, stretched, put his hands in his pockets and leaned his forehead against a doorpost.

"That helps?"

"After a few minutes."

While de Gier drank his coffee concoction Antonio frowned and concentrated.

"You know," Antonio said, "I kind of liked your

guy. I called him 'the frozen jumper.' He would stand at crossings, ready to leap, and then not move until you'd given up on him, and then he would make a giant jump and run up a path, waving and hollering. The bearded philosopher type. What did you say his name was?"

"Termeer."

Antonio' strong fingers dug about in his beard. "Termeer reminded me of the Sadguru. Are you into Hinduism at all? You've heard about the Sadguru, the Inner Teacher, He Who Won't Be Denied Ever? Your true inner self ? You can keep being stupid, fucking up and so on, but the Sadguru is getting ready."

De Gier said he was more into Buddhism.

"Okay," Antonio said. "Same thing. Call it Buddha Nature. The Relentless Force that won't put up with Ego Bullshit. That'll make you move one day in the right direction."

"I think it's called Emptiness in Buddhism," de Gier said. "I like that. The Void. You could fall into it forever."

"The Void where all the Buddhas live." Antonio nodded. He spoke solemnly. "You can't grasp Nothing. But it grasps you all right if you keep messing up. Termeer was kind of ungraspable, I thought. The other park crazies are just sick guys. Schizophrenics. Your guy looked like maybe he had it together."

"Antonio is a hopeful seeker," Freddie said. "He goes to New Age weekends." Freddie put on a stage voice. "On the mountaintop where soul-seeking men drum while growing and sharing. A hundred bucks for enlightenment; throw in another fifty and you get a semitransparent rock that holds insight."

Antonio smiled. "I get discounts." He looked serious again. "I liked Termeer's dog too. He sometimes had a dog with him, an Alsatian, a huge animal, but you know..." Antonio shook his head. "I'm confused now. That dog was with another guy. Nice guy. An older man. Well dressed. With a funny way of walking. He dragged a leg. Quite a muscular fellow otherwise."

"Two dogs?" Freddie suggested.

Antonio was thinking again.

It was pleasant in the little garden. De Gier, six hours ahead of his usual bedtime, felt the increased perception that often hit him just before falling asleep. Time seemed to slow down and Antonio's words reached him separately, clearly, floating slowly under the canopy of a Japanese maple tree.

"Same dog," Antonio said. "I know. A seeing-eye dog. Maybe the St. Nick guy and the other man shared it. But neither of those guys was blind."

"Were you in Central Park," de Gier asked, "when there was a balloon dinosaur, some gigantic beast, that kind of bobbed about, and when there was a contest of look-alike movie characters? Do you remember?"

"Yes," Antonio said.

"Did you see that man and his dog?"

Antonio thought he might have.

Chapter 12

Antonio, in his hospital whites, due to go to work at eleven, served a late breakfast in the garden. He told de Gier he was in his after-meditation "quiet mode," programmed for practical matters only. "Capers and a little chopped onion with your smoked salmon?"

"Please."

"Another poppyseed bagel?"

"Yes, thank you."

De Gier asked for a telephone. Antonio brought him a cordless model. The Japanese female clerk at the Cavendish desk said there was a problem, then connected him to the bellhop.

"This is Ignacio," the bellhop said. "*Huevones,* remember? We talked yesterday. Your friend isn't feeling good. You better come over quick. The old man was mugged. He broke his glasses."

Antonio, advising against using a taxi for such a long trip, drove de Gier to the Astor Place subway station in his gleaming restored MG sportscar. He also gave de Gier a subway token. The train was quick. De Gier, after sidestepping a woman, well dressed except for a battered straw hat, who said she had AIDS, that her name was Lisa, that she was being evicted and that she needed a hundred dollars to consult her lawyer, ran the blocks from the Eighty-sixth Street station on Lexington Avenue over to the Cavendish. He found the commissaris in his suite, sipping tea.

"Ah," the commissaris said. "They're exaggerating downstairs. Looks like I am mostly blind, though. I had multifocals, but I've lost the prescription. Katrien is express-mailing my spare pair. They'll take a few days to get here."

"Were you hurt, sir?"

The commissaris had been rattled, he reluctantly reported. The plan that day had been that, after a leisurely breakfast at Le Chat Complet, he would spend his free morning checking out Central Park, especially the area where Bert Turmeer had died. As the commissaris was approaching a cluster of bushes just east of the Sheep Meadow a jogger slowed down and fell into step with him. There was no one else in sight. The jogger was quiet.

"I am Dutch," the commissaris said, to break the silence.

"I am black," the jogger said.

The jogger suddenly hugged the commissaris, as if he were a long-lost friend. As the jogger applied pressure the commissaris's glasses slipped, fell and were stepped on. "Oh man oh man," the jogger kept shouting, "good to see you, man. How are you *doing?*"

"When did this happen, sir?" de Gier asked.

"An hour and a half ago," the commissaris said. "Maybe a little longer?"

"Can you describe your attacker?"

The commissaris did.

De Gier checked the maps Antoinette had loaned him. The Sheep Meadow was to the south; it wouldn't take him long to get there.

"But he could be anywhere now," the commissaris said. "It doesn't matter, Rinus." He raised a shoulder sadly. "It looks like I'm pretty vulnerable here, a lost cause. I'm just trouble." He looked up. "Hey? Where are you going? Rinus! Wait!"

De Gier jogged down paths south of the Great Lawn, then cruised the area around the lake. After a twenty-minute search he noted a six-foot-three-inch-tall black young adult in a sky blue sweatsuit, carrying a new white plastic shoulder bag with Adidas imprint, new ankle-high suede boots with laces, dark sunglasses in bright red frames, a pink baseball hat, wearing several big rings on the fingers of both hands, who came jogging toward him.

De Gier ran on, made a full turn, and ran after the

robber.

"I am Dutch," de Gier shouted.

The jogger was quiet.

"Oh man oh man," de Gier shouted when he was abreast of his quarry, "good to see you, man. How are you *doing?*"

The robber ran faster.

De Gier ran faster too.

The robber stopped, backed away, took a switch-blade from his bag and pressed its button. De Gier stopped too and carefully approached his opponent. The robber pointed the knife at de Gier's belly. "Fuck off, okay?"

De Gier smiled, made a pass to the right, then kicked the man's arm. He jumped the robber while the knife was still flying, got hold of a wrist, twisted it behind the man's back. He exerted some pressure.

The robber screamed.

"The money," de Gier said.

"In my back pocket, man," the robber said. "I only took sixty bucks. I left the funny money. It's still in the wallet."

De Gier pocketed the money. "What did you do with the wallet?"

"Tossed it in the garbage, man."

"Jog ahead," de Gier ordered. "Stop at the can you dumped the billfold in."

The garbage can was on Cherry Hill. The robber, after some rummaging among newspapers and empty soda cans, found the commissaris's wallet. He handed it over. De Gier thanked him.

The robber sneezed. "Give me my own money back, man. I'm sick. I got to buy some shit, man. I only took sixty."

De Gier nodded. "Fuck you, okay?"

"I'm sorry, sir," de Gier said when he returned to the Cavendish suite. "I should have checked the wallet." He grimaced. "Too hasty again. The credit card inside is made out to someone unpronounceable who lives in Trinidad and Tobago. But there's Dutch money inside. That fooled me."

"A coincidence?" the commissaris asked.

De Gier, recognizing the glint in his chief's eye, nodded. "How silly of me," de Gier said. "Where do you keep your real billfold?"

The commissaris carried his papers, valid credit card and a good deal of cash in a small armpit holster.

"The other credit card is fake," the commissaris said. "It was taken from a phony tourist. It's out of date too. Katrien told me to always let muggers have some cash, so that they won't be angry."

De Gier handed the commissaris the money he had taken from the robber.

"Two hundred dollars?" the commissaris asked. "My decoy wallet only contained sixty."

While the commissaris rested, de Gier took the surplus money to the Central Park Precinct. The desk-sergeant, who reminded de Gier of a hero out of an old war movie, a tall man in a neatly ironed blue shirt, asked, "You found a hundred and forty dollars?"

De Gier described how he happened to be following a jogger in the park. It seemed to him that the jogger was really a mugger. He had seen the jogger accost a little old gentleman, but at some distance. He couldn't be sure.

"Amazing," the desk-sergeant said.

And then later the jogger happened to drop some money.

"That belonged to the little old man?"

Yes, but that was only sixty dollars, and the sixty had been returned.

The sergeant considered. "So this money here may belong to some other victims, but nobody has filed a complaint."

"Somebody may sometime," de Gier said. "Then you can hand it over."

"Can you describe this jogger?"

De Gier did, adding that suspect, a junkie feeling sick, would undoubtedly try another mugging soon. The sergeant repeated the information into a microphone, directing the call to all park patrols. He clipped the microphone back into its holder. "What do you do, sir?"

De Gier told the sergeant he was a policeman from Amsterdam, here to assist his boss, who was unwell at the moment. His boss was the chief of detectives, Amsterdam, the Netherlands, interested in the death of a certain Bert Termeer.

"You too," the sergeant said. "I keep hearing about that case. The autopsy proved death was from natural causes. The case is being closed now. Do you want to see Sergeant Hurrell?"

De Gier wanted to see a certain mounted police-woman, just for the record, so that he could write his report. The complainant was a nephew of the deceased, a colleague in the Amsterdam Police Department.

The sergeant said, "That'll be Maggie McLaughlin. 'Mounted Maggie.'" The sergeant smiled. "She is on duty now, she'll be off for lunch. You might check here in an hour."

De Gier asked if the sergeant patrolled the park himself.

The sergeant did. Did the sergeant know of a seeing-eye dog, a large Alsatian? "What you call a German shepherd, I think."

"Kali," the sergeant said.

"Beg pardon?"

"Dog called 'Kali.'" The sergeant grinned. "Clever beast. We used to chase her—can't have unaccompanied dogs in the park—but then she adopted Charlie."

"Charlie?"

"Guy who works out in the park," the sergeant said. "A regular. We talk to each other. Fit-looking guy, muscular. Some sixty years old. Sharp dresser. Seems to have money. Pleasant disposition. Takes good care of the dog." The sergeant grinned again. "Or the other way around."

"Same dog that used to accompany our guy Termeer?"

The sergeant wasn't sure. He didn't recall Termeer. There were a lot of white-bearded men in tweeds around. Maybe he had seen him, maybe the dog had been around, maybe not. De Gier would be better off asking Policewoman Maggie.

Chapter 13

   While de Gier, killing time
as he waiting for his meeting with the policewoman,
watched polar bears swim in rhythmic circles in their
transparent quarters in the Central Park Zoo, Adjutant
Grijpstra picked up his telephone in his office at Moose
Canal Headquarters, Amsterdam.

   "Henk?" The commissaris coughed. "That you,
Adjutant?"

   Grijpstra, respectfully, took his feet off his dented
metal desk. "Sir? Are you all right? Has de Gier arrived?
How is he doing?"

   The commissaris said he himself had felt better and
that de Gier had robbed a jogger and was now turning in
part of the loot to the Central Park Precinct.

   Grijpstra slumped back until his head rested against
the wall. "You are ill and de Gier is crazy?"

"We're both fine," the commissaris said. "I am sorry about sending you on that Mad Hatter's golf errand, Henk. De Gier told me you saw the chief-constable afterward. No unpleasantness, I hope?"

Grijpstra reported.

"I wish I could say that it was my diabolical cleverness that made me nudge you into the Crailo Golf Club Alleged Murder Case," the commissaris said, "but that would only be partly true. Mostly I got my facts wrong here. No golf in Central Park, or in any public park anywhere on earth for that matter. I should have known."

Grijpstra grunted.

"You forgive me, Adjutant?" The commissaris was coughing again. He covered the telephone's mouthpiece.

"That's okay, sir."

There was a pause.

"Grijpstra?" the commissaris said, painfully shifting his aching body on his four-poster bed in the Cavendish suite. "Just to satisfy my never-ceasing curiosity, what conclusion did you reach?"

"About Baldert and his baron, sir?"

"Yes. Tell me."

"I think Baldert feels cheated out of his just punishment, sir."

"But did Baldert plan murder?"

"Probably," Grijpstra said. "And then he changed his mind at the last moment. Or he hesitated, causing some confusion, enough to make him miss the target. Then the baron died anyway and now Baldert is a madman."

"De Gier was telling me about the case," the commissaris said. "Yesterday, while eating sushi. He was getting ill again, an association with stewed eel."

Grijpstra laughed.

"De Gier thinks," the commissaris said, "that this is one of those cases where the alleged culprit seems unclear about his own guilt. To have sinned or not to have sinned, that is the question." He laughed. "How can we help?"

"How can we help ourselves to become ridiculous?" Grijpstra asked. "Baldert needs our help so that he can have his day in court. The defense asks the judge what the prosecution is talking about. The judge asks us. We don't know either. Baldert goes free, clears his conscience at the law's expense. Once again we look foolish."

"Well put," the commissaris said. "You have time to talk, Adjutant? Nellie isn't waiting with supper?"

"Nellie and I argued," Grijpstra said. "As I was wrong, again, I'm punishing myself by staying in empty cold rooms partly illuminated by a dim bulb dangling from a peeling ceiling."

"I thought you and de Gier," the commissaris said, "recently painted that ceiling."

"It's part of a poem, sir, that a Turk and I made up at a tram stop."

The commissaris was sorry to hear that Grijpstra and the Turk were depressed. He came to the point. While Grijpstra put in hmm's and ha's the commissaris argued that point. The point was that Baldert's confusion was more likely to happen in regal territories, like, for instance, The Kingdom of the Netherlands, than in an unroyal democracy like the one that the commissaris happened to be in right now. Baldert felt he had more hope if he could find royalty to judge him. What is a queen, the commissaris asked rhetorically. The queen, if not divine herself, is God's representative in the Low Countries. The mystique of the crown, Grijpstra," the commissaris declaimed. "Forefathers like our statesman Thorbecke deliberately built this bridge to beyond into our judicial system."

Grijpstra's "Hmm" showed interest.

"Our judgmental language is proof," the commissaris said. "Under our set of rules offenders can be judged to be criminally insane and referred to a mental institution 'at the queen's pleasure.' That sort of thing, Adjutant. 'At the queen's pleasure' sounds a whole lot better than 'for an indefinite period' or even, as I read in the paper here, 'for the duration.' Insert a royal person into your rules—a queen, a divine mother—and immediately there is a feeling of warmth, of divine love. It makes us look better too. As policemen we are the queen's servants. A man like Baldert wants us to lift him into a higher sphere where things finally make sense, where there is absolute good and bad, and a queen-appointed judge to tell him the difference. Baldert requires us to serve as angels." The commissaris coughed. "It would be harder to do that here."

Grijpstra professed curiosity. "Why?"

"Why, Adjutant? Because here The People judge the people."

"My God," Grijpstra said, sounding shocked.

"See?" the commissaris said. "Even you, a cynic, are appalled by such level-mindedness. Now then, Adjutant, where I really want to get to, and *am* getting to, is our alleged Central Park Murder Case. This is what I want you to do now. You and Cardozo. Maybe there is no killer but there is a much-mangled dead body. I want you to look into those body parts' background."

"I thought," Grijpstra said, "that we were all about to tentatively agree, based upon available facts, that we would tell complainant that there is no case, sir."

"The NYPD is about to close the case here," the commissaris said, "but I still feel uneasy. This time you won't be alone chasing phantoms. I want to do some background searching too. De Gier and I plan to get a certain Charlie, Termeer's landlord, to let us into Termeer's apartment and workplace. I understand the two men shared a building. We may pick up some ideas, clues, what have you, by walking about the premises where the victim lived. If I could get a better idea of how Termeer came to frolic into the azalea bushes…"

"But *why* do you feel uneasy, sir?" Grijpstra asked. "We have hard facts here. Subject habitually overexerts himself, even after open-heart surgery, a bypass and so forth. The surgery is a fact." Grijpstra waved a document at the phone. "You faxed me the autopsy, remember? The

New York coroner saw the marks. Here, right here, on official stationery...."

"Yes," the commissaris said soothingly. "I know..."

"So," Grijpstra said, "we have an old man who *frolics in parks,* which means that he runs and dances about like a madman, for God's sake. During one of these fits subject frightens a horse and is touched by its hoof. It says so, right here, sir." Grijpstra waved his own report. "...Termeer now staggers about. Passersby, reliable witnesses interviewed by de Gier and me, well-educated society folks, set him down on a park bench. Subject now seemingly recovers and is left by the Good Samaritans. However, Termeer obviously has a relapse, for his dead body is found under azalea bushes, well off the path, the next morning. So? So the old boy staggers into nearby azalea bushes, collapses, dies. What else could possibly have happened? There was nobody about by then. The entire park's population was watching events. Cause of death? Heart attack. The coroner says so."

There was some silence.

"Sir?" Grijpstra asked.

"Not all that much left for the coroner to investigate," the commissaris said. "I faxed you photographs of the corpse, Adjutant. Bits and pieces here and there. Upper parts of the thighs and the lower part of the torso are missing."

"Most of the chest was there," Grijpstra said. "The heart is in the chest. Coroner mentions a heart attack as cause of death. Isn't that all we need to know, sir?"

"Yes."

"They really have raccoons in that park, sir?"

They discussed raccoons. Grijpstra said that the raccoons released by a fur farm in Germany that Hermann Göring owned, but gave up on because of better profits in the Nazi business, had now spread into both Poland and Holland. "Maybe soon they'll arrive in our very own Vondel Park," Grijpstra said morosely. "They look cute, with those little masks on, but they're devils, sir. Raccoons get in your garbage and when you want to send them on their way they'll charge you in your own kitchen."

"Devilish denizens of the future," the commissaris said, not uncheerfully. "They won't create as much horror and terror as our species, that's for certain."

The commissaris, after cradling the phone, mused for a few moments. Was there anything in his and Grijpstra's discussion that might fit in with the persistent nightmare of the tram-driving hollow-eyed woman? Some hint that would relieve his anxiety? Hunches, parts of thoughts, even entire logical and acceptable conclusions seemed to float just under his level of consciousness.

Lying back on the springy mattress of his huge four-poster bed, the commissaris tried to concentrate. Why was he thinking that he should pay attention to something that wasn't anywhere anymore?

He drifted off into sleep again. The dream immediately produced the tram-driving Angel of Death. This time there was also chanting.

The chanting was performed by the commissaris's neighbors on Queen's Avenue, Amsterdam. The woman was Chinese, a successful artist; the man, a well-known Dutch Orientalist. The couple was Buddhist. The professor and his wife sang sutras every morning in their temple room, which was next to the commissaris's bedroom. Listening to the exotic songs had become a daily pleasure. He especially liked the "Makahanya Paramita," a term that has to do, he learned, with obtaining "Penetrating Insight." While having a Chinese fried lobster dinner with the neighbors one enjoyable evening, he was told by Suhon, the Chinese lady, that she and her learned husband opened their early-morning routine by chanting the Heart Sutra, which she called the most basic Buddhist text ever formulated. She translated a few paragraphs—the sutra was fairly brief—while she hit a small wooden hand drum to provide proper punctuation.

The lines that the commissaris remembered, when he had to wake up to go to the bathroom, were part of a dialogue between Avalokitasavara, a bodhisattva, who returns from his meditations in high realms, and Sariputra, a less-developed Buddha-spirit.

As the sutra is outlined further the bodhisattva dominates the stage. Avalokitasavara wants to share with his pupil his basic discovery:

Sariputra, form is not other than emptiness
and emptiness is not other than form
form is precisely emptiness
and emptiness precisely form

Beautiful, the commissaris thought. So now what? So now *not* what? He liked the idea of emptiness. If something isn't there, one doesn't have to worry about maintaining or protecting it. The two spirits were active on higher levels, however. The commissaris, from his lowly position as an incarnate human, could only see the empty aspects of his case, the loopholes. How to turn them around and give the bits of void form?

"Imagine the missing piece," the commissaris told his mirror image in the bathroom, "right here. On your lower level."

Chapter 14

"Mounted Maggie," as the desk sergeant called her, was late coming from duty. As she strode into the precinct's front room she seemed pleasantly surprised to see de Gier. "Are you the foreign policeman?"

De Gier shared her feelings. Maggie was a good—also intelligent—looking woman. He explained his presence. She looked less pleased. "The old freeze and frolic man. I called him Fritz. Fritz won't go away, will he? Did you see those terrible photos?" She shook her head in disgust. "The Urban Rangers say raccoons are a plague now. Never see them myself; the varmints mostly move at night. We should hunt them with hounds and flashlights like they do in the country."

Maggie's ponytail bobbed as she walked next to him. "And you came all the way from Amsterdam? What *is* so special about the old man?"

De Gier suggested lunch but Maggie was still in uniform and wanted to go home and change. Home was on West Twelfth Street, where she shared an apartment with another female "mountie." She asked questions as he walked her to her car, a battered enclosed jeep parked behind the building on the Eighty-fifth Street transverse. So he was only staying a few days. So he knew no one but his superior at the Cavendish Hotel ("But that's a thousand bucks a day. Is your chief connected?"). So he wasn't married—did he have a boyfriend? No? Did he like sports? Judo? Really? And where was he staying?

Their addresses were close. She dropped him off at Fourteenth Street and Eight Avenue. She touched his arm as he got out of the jeep. "You like Italian food? Can you find your way around? Want to meet me in SoHo? Prince and Sullivan Streets, in an hour?"

He walked over to the restaurant, worrying. The carefree days were over, he didn't feel at ease with attractive women who signaled welcome. Did she think Europeans were exciting lovers? He should have told her he was married. She probably expected him to perform. Keep it up for some record period. Do weird stuff like sucking toes while she played French harmonica music on a CD.

De Gier felt sleepy. He had a vision of his quiet Horatio Street rooms. He could open the windows there and listen to birds singing. Have tea. Play Miles Davis through his earphones. Take a nap.

Walking down Greenwich Avenue he was stared at by men in black leather, in safari suits, in riding breeches and oversize linen shirts, in bib overalls and back-to-front caps. De Gier stopped consulting his street map to avoid offers to show him the way "to wherever you may be going, Mistah Macho. You're from out of town?"

"No, thank you," de Gier told a bodybuilder in a straw hat, an Indonesian sepia-colored vest and short shorts. "I think I know where I am going."

Maggie, looking gorgeous, he thought, sedately sexy in a close-fitting flowerprinted dress, was waiting in the restaurant. The restaurant was decorated with posters advertising Fellini films and tall plants with large leaves. The furniture was heavy pine, varnished. Rustic looking. The waiters wore aprons and bow ties and seemed to like walking with one hand behind their backs. While he checked twenty-dollar specials on the blackboard Maggie told him she felt awkward about Termeer: "I could have done better."

When she saw he was having trouble understanding the menu she translated the names of some of the fancier spaghetti sauces. "My ex-husband is an Italian cook. Our schedules were always wrong, we hardly ever saw each other. It's easy to drift apart in this town."

Any kids?

No kids.

Was de Gier ever married?

No.

Any particular reason?

Because of the things, de Gier explained while they shared the antipasto. It wasn't just marriage, it was that marriage comes with the need to collect things, and the need to worry about losing things. Things weigh heavily. There is monthly interest. There is anxiety.

"You can't handle marriage?"

De Gier couldn't handle marriage.

Maggie looked up from her black olives. "You don't want kids?"

"In Holland?" de Gier asked. "What if they don't want to be stacked on top of each other? Where am I going to put them? In a hole in a dike? What if they don't want to stay stacked? I don't want to myself."

"Where do you want to go?"

To Papua New Guinea, to the furthest place. She wouldn't know where that was.

"North of Australia," Maggie said. "My sister sails in that area, to Milne Bay out of Brisbane. Her husband owns a schooner. They take tourists for big dough. There are pirate cannibals there, Papuans in canoes, with razor-sharp paddles."

That's where de Gier wanted to go.

"To have room for your kids?"

Just a dog maybe. De Gier hadn't owned a dog yet. He would like to try that.

"They eat dogs there," Maggie said. "It said so in

Kathleen's last letter. The cannibals keep dogs for food. There is no refrigeration, so if the family wants meat for dinner Pa picks up a stick and chases Fido. But they don't eat their kids. You would get to keep them."

He didn't want to keep them.

"But you look fine," Maggie said. "You look smart too. You might improve the gene pool."

He muttered, as he raised his tumbler filled with the house wine, dry white California, "*Fok* the gene pool."

She laughed. "You have a cute accent. It's okay. I don't want kids either. I thought I did but kids keep killing each other at school now. So are you an egotist? Incapable of sharing?"

De Gier said that he did like his cat, now being taken care of by friends.

"So you have friends? You socialize?"

De Gier looked horrified. "You mean do I visit with people?"

"You don't do that?"

"To do what?"

"You're not gay?"

De Gier shook his head. "I keep busy."

"You're a ladies' man?" She smiled. "You cruise the singles bars?" She smiled again. "But you wouldn't have to, would you? You don't want them to fall in love with you, to jump at you from their high horses."

Jesus, de Gier thought. *Any*body up there. Please.

Maggie was shaking her head. "There is old age, you

know, and loneliness."

He waved defensively. "I know. We are programmed to be gregarious."

"You know why I became a mountie?" Maggie asked. "To stay away from what is happening now. To look down on things. I was a street cop first. I did everything—cars, a motorcycle even—and I always managed to find old people in their little apartments, always alone, always dying or dead or just disgusting. The linoleum is always cracked and sometimes the walls move because of the roaches crawling on roaches and there are the smells, rusted-through refrigerators filled with *yechch*"—she gestured—"rats rattling in useless dishwashers...."

He knew. It was the same in Amsterdam but there they're short on dishwashers. Not on rats. He had seen rats jump to get at the dead canary in the cage.

All the gruesome details.

De Gier's sensitive large brown eyes looked into Maggie's sensitive slanting green eyes.

"So?" Maggie asked.

He grinned. "So what. There's always death at the end. Death never seems to be pleasant. Birth isn't fun either, but there is the quest in between."

He became flirtatious for a moment. "There is the beautiful company."

Maggie said thank you. "You look okay too. Is that mustache real?"

He brought up Termeer again over mochacinos

topped with whipped cream.

"I thought I was done with finding dead old people, that Jagger would lift me out of the misery. He's a nice tall horse." Maggie smiled. He noticed her lips, the sort of lips that could advertise lipstick. "Jagger didn't help at all. On the contrary. Jagger almost hurt Fritz. Jagger, being such a large horse, is usually calm but Fritz was standing still again, looking like Mercury...."

"Mercury?" de Gier asked.

She nodded. "The Roman god. The messenger pose. There's a statue of Mercury on top of one of the buildings way downtown, I don't remember where. A nude guy with one leg up, one arm forward, one arm backward, head raised, winged hat?"

De Gier had slipped into his sympathetic questioning mode. "Yes, the pose must be tiring."

"Your old codger was able to hold it pretty well." Maggie grimaced. "Fritz had Jagger fooled. I think animals have trouble seeing objects that don't move. So suddenly Fritz started running about like some hyped-up toddler. You can't really blame Jagger. Why did Fritz have to spoil such a nice Sunday? We were all having fun." She stared through de Gier, transported back to Central Park that sunny morning. She told him about the wonderful balloon structure, the huge dinosaur, moving every which way in the breeze, making all the kids scream when the big head dipped toward them, and there were the Park Stompers with their Dixieland tunes and old blues, and the movie-character look-alikes on their way to the contest, and suddenly there is horror. Up pops Fritz.

De Gier looked sympathetic.

"Jagger's hoof just grazed him," Maggie said. "I dismounted to check whether he was okay. He kept saying he was fine, not to bother."

Maggie frowned. "I apologized, I even offered to get an ambulance. That's a big no-no, you know, a police horse damaging a civilian. I was prepared to call the precinct on my radio, get someone higher up to check out the scene." She shook her head again. "But Fritz said he was fine."

"No nausea, no shock, nothing?"

Maggie's ponytail swung both ways. "He said he was just fine."

"Then what happened?"

Maggie remembered an old tourist couple, with the same accent as de Gier's, harassing her. She had ridden off but the couple called her back. Fritz was sitting on a bench by that time. He looked a bit tired. She didn't feel like talking to him again and had ordered the couple "on their way."

"That's where I went wrong," Maggie said. "Fritz wasn't okay." Maggie's ponytail bobbed about again. "The investigation at the precinct exonerated me, but I don't feel good about not going back."

De Gier asked about the seeing-eye dog called Kali.

Maggie thought she had seen the dog that Sunday,

possibly with a man called Charlie. An older man, muscular, who worked out in the playgrounds. "He drags one leg, but not too badly. He should use a cane."

Maggie didn't know whether Fritz and Charlie knew each other.

She might have seen the dog with Fritz, she couldn't remember. Kali often roamed around by herself, which was prohibited. Dogs were supposed to be on a leash. She had talked to Charlie about that but you know what they're like. "Yes, ma'am…fuck you, ma'am."

Would Charlie say that?

No, he would think that.

Yes, Maggie said now, she was fairly sure she had seen Charlie and the dog on the day Fritz was grazed by the hoof of her horse, Jagger.

After the meal—she insisted on separate checks— they walked about. The weather was pleasant. She walked him along Prince and Spring Streets to look at windows displaying art. They had fancy coffees in a West Broadway café. By five o'clock she took him to a videotape rental store.

"Are you free tonight?"

He used the store's phone to reach the Cavendish. The commissaris was lying down after attending his lecture. "You're still with the mounted lady, Sergeant?"

"I can come back," de Gier said hopefully. "Didn't you want to check out Tribeca tonight, where Termeer used to live?"

The commissaris had managed to reach Charlie, after getting a telephone number from Chief O'Neill. "Tomorrow evening, Sergeant. You have tonight off. Enjoy yourself. Keep that lady talking. We might learn something more."

"Are you feeling all right, sir?"

The commissaris felt somewhat better. He would just rest. Try to get his temperature down. The bellhop Ignacio had lent him a book by a Mexican crime writer, "*No Happy Ending*, by Ignacio Paco Taibo II. A relevant title, Sergeant."

"A Mexican writing in English?"

The commissaris picked up the paperback. "Translated. It's good. The Mexican background makes it even more interesting. Well written too. Would you like to read it in Spanish? Ignacio says there is a Spanish bookstore here. Maybe he should get you a copy."

De Gier sounded tired. "I don't read mysteries."

"Snob." The commissaris raised a correcting finger. "You're missing out on exercises in morality, the tension between libido and superego, the search for essential values—if any, of course—comparisons in relativity, the different, often conflicting, mores of sociologically separated groups, psychological insights, animal studies and tribal customs, the concept of the police as a uniformed mafia, the use of magic in crime..."

"Taibo brings up all that?"

The commissaris patted the book. "Some, Sergeant.

Some. Quite a bit in fact. There is some connection to our case there, I think, but I haven't finished the novel."

"*No Happy Ending?* You think our case is not going to end well, sir?"

The commissaris coughed.

"But if you have a fever," de Gier said, "maybe I should come over."

"Just a touch," the commissaris said. "You enjoy yourself. You can come over for breakfast."

"Yes," de Gier said unhappily.

He hung up. "I am free."

"Good." Maggie grinned. "Want to see a movie? My roommate won't be in tonight, she is staying over with her mom in Brooklyn."

Maggie's favorite star was Mel Gibson. She and de Gier checked through the store's stock together. She recommended *The Year of Living Dangerously*, and de Gier said he would like to see that but then he picked up *The Road Warrior* and read the cover. Bizarre—Action—The Australian Outback—Surrealistic.

"You want to see that?"

De Gier tried to remember who liked bizarre, surrealistic Australian Outback adventure movies. Johan Termeer. De Gier didn't think he shared young Termeer's tastes. The man was a hairdresser. Gay, too. But also a policeman. Tough. Someone who would take on a Yugoslavian gangster. De Gier hesitated. Why see a dubious movie if there were good movies around? This was Woody Allen country, he had never seen *Manhattan*.

Maggie said she couldn't possibly see *Manhattan* again. She rented *The Road Warrior*. "Good action. I don't mind seeing it again. You'll love it." She laughed. "There's a couple doing it in a tent, and a car roars up and whips off their cover. You should see their faces. And there is a guy eating dog food from a can in a dead tree while he watches the enemy through an old brass telescope. My kid brother was inspired by that scene. He found a telescope too and a crate of Alpo and the fire brigade had to pry him out of a tree."

Chapter 15

"The commissaris wants to know about Termeer's background," Adjutant Grijpstra told Detective-Constable-First-Class Simon Cardozo. "The man left this country twenty years ago. For America. Never came back. You're a bright young man, Cardozo. Where do we start?"

Cardozo smirked. "Maybe Termeer played golf?"

Grijpstra patted Cardozo's arm. "You're still annoyed you weren't in on the Crailo Golf Club expedition?"

"I might have pointed out that there is no golf playing in Central Park," Cardozo said. "Furthermore, I would have…"

"Bert Termeer's background," Grijpstra hollered, "you've read the file. I want you to suggest something. Okay?" Grijpstra swung hairy fists over Cardozo's head. He dropped the hairy fists and spoke gently. "Okay."

"Okay," Cardozo said.

"What do we do?" Grijpstra whispered.

Cardozo combed his tousled hair with his fingers. "Find someone who knew old Bert Termeer."

"The Younger Termeer," Grijpstra said, while checking de Gier's notes on his interview with Termeer's nephew. "Old Termeer had a girlfriend, a certain Carolien, his landlady...hmmm...didn't share beds, did they?...had their own quarters...she liked having sex with the mailman and somesuch..." He looked across the room at Cardozo. "What to you make of that?"

"Maybe an intellectual relationship?" Cardozo asked. "But the lady is dead. Remember? Suicide due to advanced multiple sclerosis?"

Grijpstra wanted positive input.

"Who do we know," Cardozo asked brightly, "who knew Bert Termeer, who isn't dead?"

There was only Jo Termeer, the nephew. Jo Termeer had been questioned by de Gier. The object of that interview was to determine the seriousness of complaint's request. There had been no emphasis on the dead man's past.

"I'll phone," Cardozo said.

Grijpstra checked his watch. "Food first."

They walked over to a sandwich shop nearby at Rose Canal. While Grijpstra ordered shrimp and smoked eel on white buns, soft, hold the onions, no mayo on his French fries, coffee with, Cardozo used a pay phone.

Jo Termeer picked up.

"Good evening, this is Detective-Constable Cardozo. A few routine questions, please. You aren't busy?"

Jo was busy.

"This won't take a minute. It's about your uncle."

Jo said that he had told de Gier everything he knew. He suggested Cardozo replay the tape.

"Your uncle was a member of the bookdealers' society?"

Jo didn't know.

"Hobbies?" Cardozo asked. "No? Affiliation with a church or an investment society? No? He dealt in spiritual books, right? Any Buddhist or Hindu contacts? No? Freemasons, Rosicrucians, Rotarians, theosophical, anthroposophical, astrological interests, associations, friends? No?

"Liked to visit a specific café?

"Relatives anywhere, except you, of course?"

"Not that I know of," Jo said. "Goodbye." He hung up.

Cardozo entered the sandwich shop to tell the adjutant that, in his opinion, Jo Termeer was an asshole.

Grijpstra and Cardozo ate the last shrimp the owner said he would ever serve. Now that the North Sea was being fished out, the shop's customers could no longer afford the price. A minimal wholesale order was a bushel. Freezer shelf life was limited. Invest a fortune to eventually feed rats and sea gulls?

The owner wrote the bill and pushed it across his marble counter. "I'm sorry, gents. Order beef tongue next time."

"You still live with your parents, Cardozo," Grijpstra said after reading the total. "You pay."

Cardozo peeled off large brightly colored banknotes.

"And *I* should have phoned young Termeer," Grijpstra said. "You probably used your high-pitched phone voice again. It irritates the other party."

"Adjutant," Cardozo pleaded, "we're trying to *help* the fellow."

"Poor fellow had a bad day," Grijpstra said. "Young Termeer's client burned his pompadour in the dryer. Or it was dyed the wrong color maybe. Bastard wouldn't pay, raised a ruckus. Wanted Termeer to pay *him* maybe. Charged negligence or whatnot. And in the midst of all that misery you squeak in his ear."

"Here we go all out," Cardozo said, "trying to solve the asshole's problem, and he won't answer simple questions?"

Grijpstra pleaded. "I know him. I taught the man. One year at police school. Three evenings a week. I tell you, Simon, subject is attentive, correct, has a pleasant attitude, is willing to cooperate...."

"Please." Cardozo shrugged. "As a student he was motivated to show his better side. He wanted to be a policeman. You were the instructor. You would be grading his papers."

"You're right." Grijpstra pushed Cardozo into the street. "Everybody is right. *Nellie* is right." He was raising his voice.

They walked around a large squatting dog. Grijpstra growled at the dog. "Don't do that, it's illegal, where is your boss? Does he have his prescribed shovel and plastic bags? Do you know what the fine is for doing what you're doing?"

The dog growled back.

Cardozo waved at a member of the municipal brigade of Mechanized On-the-Spot Cleaners, which patrols Amsterdam's inner city. The smartly uniformed man rode his gleaming white motorcycle over. He maneuvered it between the penis-shaped cast-iron posts that are set into the edges of sidewalks to prevent illegal parking. "What do we have here?" The cleaner saluted the dog. "Aha." The man pointed the shiny nozzle of his vacuum tube at the squatting dog's backside. He held his finger on the handgrip's trigger.

"Switch it on," Grijpstra said, but the dog wasn't done yet. It looked over its shoulder, baring large sharp canines.

"This thing is powerful," the cleaner shouted over the Kawasaki's steady reverberations. "It could rip out the dog's ass."

The dog, done now, barked happily and loped off. "There we go," the cleaner said. He pulled the trigger behind the tube's nozzle. The vacuum's tube sucked loudly. There was a rumble in the cylinder welded to his luggage carrier.

The sidewalk was clean again, its cobblestones shining mysteriously in late sunlight.

"Big fellows like that scare me," the cleaner said, "although the work is more rewarding. Little dogs are okay. If they're real little I don't wait till they're done." He laughed. "If they fit into the tube...upsadaisy!"

The Kawasaki roared off.

"He was kidding, right?" Cardozo asked.

Grijpstra marched on. "We know that Bert Termeer once operated a street stall in Old Man's Gate on Old Side Canal. Let's ask around. Maybe some oldtimer will remember." He showed his electronic watch to Cardozo. "Can't read this without glasses. It *is* Thursday?"

Amsterdam retail outlets stay open on Thursday evenings.

The detectives caught a streetcar to Dam Square and walked via Dam Street and Old Side Canal to Old Man's Gate book market, a long corridor between ancient gray buildings at the beginning of the Red Light District crescenting St. Nicholas Church.

Tourists and students crowded between the corridor's ornate iron gates, around trestle tables bending under stacks of reading matter. Cardozo leafed through a British Victorian art book. It showed etchings of lesbian positions. Grijpstra talked to a seller operating under a large sign that said "Bieber Birds." The old stooped dealer resembled a bird himself: a great crested blue heron on long thin legs, with a sharp beaklike nose.

Mr. Bieber remembered his colleague Bert Termeer well.

Grijpstra explained his interest after showing his police card. "An inquiry on behalf of the family. Mr. Termeer died in Central Park in New York under not really suspicious circumstances. Heart trouble probably. This is merely routine."

Oh yes, bookseller Bieber knew all about bad health. On your feet in a drafty passage all day—it was amazing he himself hadn't succumbed as yet. Of course he himself lived as restful a life as circumstances permitted. Termeer's lifestyle was always exhausting. The man had spent long hours buying and selling his so-called spiritual books, and then, evenings, during the weekend and so forth, holidays, what have you, hot summer evenings when most people relax, Termeer would be out there in the city, performing his act in front of cafés.

"Act?"

Bieber nodded. "Bone diving, he called it."

Cardozo, at the next table, studying voluptuous female bodies united by dildos, looked up. "A sexual connotation?"

Bieber tittered. "Bone, not boner."

Grijpstra was bewildered. "Termeer dived for bones?"

Bieber said he hadn't understood the term either at

first. Termeer's signboard above his table in the Gate said "Bone Diver." It had worried Bieber when Termeer started out. "Divers" are birds, and Bieber wanted no competition, certainly not from a table that adjoined his own.

But it was okay. Termeer dealt in so-called spiritual books, with a sideline of erotica.

"Erotica?"

Bieber gestured appeasingly. "Young acrobats and wrestlers running about. Greek stuff. Pastoral scenes. Little kids cavorting. Girls in the bathtub. All playful-like. Invigorating." Bieber rubbed his hands. "Kept him going, he said."

"Porno?"

"Nah." Bieber waved the accusation away. "You mean the hard stuff? You won't find that in the Gate. Termeer sold so-called spiritual stuff mostly."

Grijpstra raised his heavy steel-wool eyebrows. "So what's the bone-diving bullshit?"

Bieber shrugged. "Something mystical maybe?"

"A koan," Cardozo said. "Like in Zen. Some strangely phrased riddle. There's lots of allegory here." He pointed at the corridor's gates. "Pass through the gates of learning, dive for bones of wisdom."

"My erudite assistant was selected for intelligence," Grijpstra said to Bieber. "To me this sounds farfetched."

Bieber said farfetched terms attract the curious. People would come over to ask Termeer about his giant carved-in-oak sign, hanging from squeaky chains above the table loaded with Eastern wisdom. Yoga and so forth. Buddhism. The Tao. The meaning of Sufi dances.

"No Christian material?"

Bieber said, "Maybe early Christian. Nothing simple." He scowled. "But Termeer never explained anything." He cheered up again. "Termeer's acting aimed at making you guess what he was up to. So people would look at me, behind the next table, paying attention to what Termeer was going to pull, and ask me about this 'diver' thing and I'd get a chance to show my waterfowl pictures.

"Like this, see?" Bieber opened a picture book and turned pages. "Here. Know what these are?"

Cardozo tried. "Giant uncrested grebes?"

Bieber tittered again. "Wiseass. You, sir?"

Grijpstra thought the birds were sea geese.

Bieber nodded. "Red-throat divers, pearl divers, ice divers—not too many of those left nowadays—yellow-beaked divers. No bone divers, but what the hell." He winked. "Thing is to get clients interested. You don't want to stand around passive-like all the time. Got to pull 'em in and make them buy. Get some action. Most folks like to buy bird pictures." Bieber waved his coat sleeves like a heron waves its wings before stumbling into flight. "Birds are special."

"Apart from refusing to explain his bone diver sign," Grijpstra asked, "what else did your colleague do to attract attention?"

"He was different," Bieber said. "Altogether." He looked hopefully at the adjutant, as if expecting understanding from a peer. "You know?"

Grijpstra knew, but he wanted Bieber to expand his knowledge.

Bieber's theory, based on observations made during years of watching Termeer's antics, ruled out craziness. The used-book trade is too marginal to allow for madness. Bieber therefore theorized that Termeer fit the "surrealist niche."

Bieber showed his false teeth in a helpful smile. "Fitting regular things together differently to get something different across? Different knowledge?"

Grijpstra was patient. "So what regular things did Termeer fit together differently, Mr. Bieber?"

"Like how?" Cardozo asked.

"Well," Bieber said, "there was the sign, there were the animals.

"Termeer," Bieber continued, "owned a mongrel that was so smart he knew when to look stupid. The dog would grab people by their coats and drag them over to Termeer's trestle table.

"There was also the macaque." Bieber liked the dog but he never cared for the monkey. Monkeys defecate anywhere. This one preferred bird books.

"The monkey brought in clients too?"

Bieber nodded. The macaque danced ahead of

people and pulled faces and pointed at the so-called spiritual books.

So Bert Termeer invented ways to get through to people to impart different knowledge?

"Right," Bieber said. Termeer would insult his clients. He might recommend books and then refuse to sell them, charge outrageously, even tear books up. He might give a book away and then run after the client and try to get it back.

"Lots of funny old ladies hanging around that table, I bet," Grijpstra said.

No, Bieber said. Bert Termeer wouldn't deal with so-called spiritual old ladies. He would shoo them away.

"And he still sold well?"

Oh yes, Bieber said. People would come from all over. Americans. British. There was the mail-order side too. His catalogue did well.

Cardozo interrupted. "You keep saying 'so-called' spiritual, sir. You mean...?"

"Listen," Bieber winked, beckoning Cardozo closer, "can anyone write, print, read the truth about meaning? Or origin? Or the future? Or the present for that matter?" Bieber cackled diabolically. "You want peace of mind?" Bieber squeezed Cardozo's cheek. "Can the mind be peaceful? Aren't minds filled with thoughts? You want to read in more thoughts?"

Bieber pointed his beaklike nose at the sky and flapped his sleeves, looking more like a heron than ever.

"That's the infinite out there. The great secret." He poked a wing at Cardozo. "You think you can put infinity into books?"

Grijpstra said, "But that was Termeer's living. He lived a lie?"

"Who doesn't?" Bieber asked.

So how to become truthful? Bieber asked Bieber.

Maybe by creating seemingly crazy circumstances, Bieber answered Bieber. By creating a crack in the regular world regular folks build up for themselves. Then slip through it.

"Through the crack?"

"Yessir," Bieber said.

"Into what?"

"Reality."

"And what so-called spiritual exercises did Termeer himself engage in to become real, Mr. Bieber?" Grijpstra asked patiently.

Bieber frowned.

"Not so so-called?"

"Not the exercises," Bieber said.

"And those were?"

Bieber became hesitant. "I told you. Termeer would wander about the city, evenings and weekends, searching for the right moments, the right locations."

"To do this bone diving?" Cardozo asked.

Bieber's eyes were half closed, his arms moved slowly, as he seemed to enter a trance.

"Mr. Bieber, you okay?"

Grijpstra held up a hand, to silence Cardozo.

"Termeer played good trumpet," Bieber said after a while. "He would set himself up facing a terrace filled with people. He would have his dog on one side and the monkey on the other. The monkey would be dressed up in a robe and a hat. Then Termeer would play his trumpet. Some fine jazz phrasing. Like Louis Armstrong; maybe 'St. Louis Blues,' maybe 'Basin Street Blues,' that sort of thing."

"That's nice," Cardozo said.

Bieber nodded. "A fine sense of the dramatic. And then, once he had the public's attention he might talk for a while, asking them how they were doing, making a few odd remarks, disconnected. The monkey would go around, grimacing and jabbering. People might offer him money and the little beast would bow and back off. No money for the monkey. The dog would bark commas and question marks, a semicolon here and there. After that Termeer usually played his trumpet again.

"This was long ago, mind you. Cops still wore brass helmets and little sabers. A cop would come up and ask Bieber for his license, and then…"

Bieber laughed. "Haha, the dog would be standing behind the cop, and the monkey would sit on Termeer's shoulder with his hands behind his ears and tongue out, chattering, infuriating the copper, and then Termeer would push—"

Bieber clapped his hands. "The cop would fall over backward, the dog would run off, Bieber and the monkey would step into a passing tram car—they still had running boards in those days—the dog would be waiting at the next stop and everyone would go home." Bieber looked triumphant. "And be happy. The public too. You should have been there."

Grijpstra and Cardozo thanked Mr. Bieber. They were about to walk away.

Grijpstra turned. "Last question, Mr. Bieber," Grijpstra said. "There is a nephew, Jo Termeer, partly raised by Bert Termeer. Did you get to know the nephew?"

Bieber vaguely recalled a boy coming to Old Man's Gate, calling Bert "uncle." Not too often.

The boy seemed shy.

"There was a good relationship between uncle and nephew?"

"Sure," Bieber said. "Yes, I think so. Why not?"

Chapter 16

De Gier, after a tour of the Village and dinner at a Chinese fast-food place, was taken to Maggie's apartment on Twelfth Street. Maggie apologized for the apartment's appearance. She knew it was dreary but it belonged to her roommate and nobody liked housework.

"We do clean occasionally though."

"You eat here?" de Gier asked.

"Hardly ever. In the morning maybe. I put a frozen waffle in the toaster." She patted her flat stomach. "Today I binged. That means dieting for a week."

She switched on the TV, told him to sit on a beige plastic couch with factory-embroidered pink cushions in each corner, handed over a large remote control and went off to shower and change. A newscaster appeared, adjusted his cuffs, bowed and dramatically recited headlines. They all sounded bad. De Gier pressed the remote's mute button. The first clip was war: He watched hungry-looking soldiers in summer uniforms getting shot at in a winter landscape. A beautiful woman in an off-the-shoulder dress danced about a cruise ship where fat men laughed as impeccable waiters heaped more food on their plates. The newscaster reappeared to smile briefly. Old folks in a home were beaten by their attendants. A hidden camera showed the pictures in black and white. The black-and-white old people screamed soundlessly as leering attendants forced them to sign papers. The newscaster nodded. A beautiful woman ate breakfast cereal on a terrace overlooking a lake. She closed her eyes and showed the tip of her tongue after daintily chewing her crispy breakfast. The newscaster smiled, then faded as the screen was filled by a burning bus under palm trees, then by mangled bodies of children at the side of the road. The newscaster came back. De Gier read his lips. "More news in a moment." A compact car looking like any other compact, but clean and polished, was driven by a beautiful woman in an evening gown and gloves up to her elbows. The woman pursed her lips as if waiting for a kiss while she made her vehicle accelerate effortlessly in an empty city street. More newscaster's smiles before a two-story house slid down a hill's steep slope towards cars buried up to their roofs in mud.

De Gier pressed the remote's power button.

He stretched out on the couch and tried to rest his

eyes by looking at a bouquet of silk roses in a bright green vase on a mirrored coffee table, then turned on his back so that he could look at the ceiling.

Maggie woke him up. "You snore."

It was two hours later.

De Gier sat up and apologized. "Why didn't you wake me?"

"You probably have jet lag. I thought you needed rest but you were making such a racket. Were you choking on your mustache?"

She had made gin and tonics decorated with slices of orange.

They toasted each other.

De Gier told her the snoring might be due to a recent operation. His nose had been damaged during an arrest some years ago and hadn't healed well. A surgeon broke it again to open up the left nostril. Both nostrils were sometimes blocked now. He would have to go back. Maybe have another operation.

She was interested. "When did this happen?"

He tried to remember. "Two months ago?"

"You don't know exactly?" She looked concerned.

De Gier laughed.

She stirred her gin and tonic. "What's so funny?"

"Nothing," de Gier said. "But before an operation a hospital will check a patient's blood. If there is AIDS it will inform the patient."

"So you were clean," Maggie said.

He wasn't sure. The AIDS virus takes sixty days to become visible in testing.

"And you had been active within the sixty days before your nose job?"

He had been active.

Maggie sighed. "So have I."

She stood looking down at him. "My guy is married. A safe and solid kind of a guy. His wife has lymph cancer. He can't divorce her."

"Ah," de Gier said.

"So you were active with what kind of person?"

"With a prostitute," de Gier said. "Kind of high class. The type that is careful."

Maggie said prostitution was illegal. She knew cops who protected prostitutes, so they got free service.

De Gier said prostitution was legal in Holland. He had paid. Maggie liked that. Nobody likes to give free service. "Am I right?"

"You are right," de Gier said.

"You sure you paid?"

He nodded. "Top guilder."

"You do that often?"

De Gier said he did not. Once during three months. He was getting older.

"And you don't have girlfriends?"

He shook his head. "They always want to get married."

"Yes," Maggie said. "We can't always ride tall

horses." She poured more gin, pushed *The Road Warrior* into her VCR and sat down next to de Gier on the beige plastic couch.

During the movie, which he liked, he was aware of her body in the semitransparent robe. She had untied her ponytail. He thought she looked very inviting and attractive.

She stopped the movie when de Gier said he'd like to see the man in longjohns fly his machine again, "or whatever it was, the thing with the blade." He also had to go to the bathroom. "Take a shower," Maggie said. "Wrap yourself in a towel afterward. I put out a huge one. You can shave too if you like. There is gear next to the washstand; there's nice aftershave, too."

"I could see you as Road Warrior," Maggie said when he came back, "in leather, and with that riot gun pistol, and the boots, driving hot rods across endless deserts. The lonely hero to be comforted by the lady in white."

She had refilled their glasses. They both began to slur their words while commenting on the movie's final and spectacular battle between odd-looking automobiles. Maggie was sad when the lady in white, who manipulated a flame thrower from the top of a tank truck driven by Mel Gibson, was killed by an arrow.

"If that was me, we couldn't do it."

The movie ended. Maggie led de Gier to her bedroom. His towel slipped off. Her robe slipped off too.

"Don't we look nice?" Maggie whispered.

He thought they might have just one more drink.

When she came back with the refilled glasses he asked whether she had seen a Road Warrior look-alike in the park the day that Bert Termeer got killed.

"I sure did," Maggie said. "It should have been you."

"How many?"

"Just one." She laughed. "Should have been two and you would have been the other and you would have done something bad and I would have arrested you and dragged you along behind me."

De Gier made himself smile at that S&M scene. "Did you see him from close by?"

"No." She leaned over to kiss his cheek and sniffed the aftershave. "My favorite. Herbal. You like herbal?"

De Gier didn't. "Sure."

"I was on my horse," Maggie said. "I had to be everywhere. There were all these kids. Falling in the pond. Trying to prick holes in the balloons of the dinosaur. There was that loud tuba thumping that makes Jagger prance and rear."

They sat on the double bed, sipping their gins, admiring each other's bodies. She complimented him on his wide chest. He complimented her on her beautiful bosom.

They put their drinks down and lay back, just to relax for a moment, before getting "serious," Maggie said.

He went back to the bathroom, where he had left his

clothes.

"You brought a condom?" Maggie asked. "How thoughtful." She frowned. "Always ready, eh?" Her smile came back. "Shall I put it on?" She touched him and laughed at the prompt reaction. "Instant hydraulics!"

"Powerful." She played some more, too roughly. The condom broke. "You think it is all right?" she asked. "I am wearing something."

He thought it might be all right. He didn't sound sure.

Her hand slipped away. They lay back again, not touching.

His eyelids dropped. He was snoring again, and she turned him on his side and made her breasts caress his shoulder so that he would wake up, which he did, but then she dozed off herself.

The palms of his hands rubbed her breasts lightly. What beautiful duplicity. How generous of nature to multiply such a perfectly firm and smooth living shape. He lifted his hands, then touched one breast, then the other. "Two," de Gier murmured dreamily, then he frowned, thinking about being the second Road Warrior, being dragged to Twelfth Street by a horse.

Good twos, bad twos.

Two Road Warriors in Central Park.

Chapter 17

De Gier, breakfasting late with a somewhat rested commissaris at the Cavendish the next day, was handed Grijpstra's and Cardozo's faxed report on the visit to Old Man's Gate. The document had been delivered by the bellhop Ignacio to the commissaris's suite together with his morning coffee and his spare glasses, brought over by a courier at considerable expense.

The commissaris couldn't see well, as the spare glasses had been manufactured ten years ago according to a much weaker prescription.

He complained about have bad dreams again. "About a streetcar driver."

"What did he do, sir?"

"It was a she."

"What did she do?"

"I think she wanted me to deliver something." The commissaris took off his useless glasses and stared hopelessly at de Gier. "All legs, no eyes." He waved. "Never mind. Read that report, Sergeant. Let's catch up with the homefront."

De Gier read aloud while the commissaris cut kiwis and arranged the slices on his yogurt.

"More juice?" the commissaris asked. "Try grapefruit this time. Another aspirin? Feeling better?"

De Gier felt worse but he was forcing himself to pay attention. "What do you think, sir?"

The commissaris was done thinking. De Gier was in charge. The commissaris had another lecture that day, on homemade lethal weapons. Chief O'Neill would pick him up in an hour. He was still interested in the Termeer case, of course. He was more than willing to hear about de Gier's progress.

De Gier suggested that, on the strength of the report from Amsterdam, Jo Termeer might be a suspect.

The commissaris, while buttering a crisp white bun, investigated his choice of cheeses. "You see possibilities that weren't available to us before?"

De Gier argued that Bert Termeer—according to Bieber and to Sara Lakmaker, who had only met Termeer briefly, and to Antonio, partner of de Gier's Horatio Street landlord, Freddie—was a charismatic figure, a latter-day prophet. Prophets, by definition, spend their time and energy trying to share uncommon and beneficial insights.

They may use odd methods.

"Tell me about Antonio," the commissaris said.

De Gier reported. "He sails model boats in Central Park, sir. He has seen old Termeer stand still and jump about. 'The prophet' impressed him. There has even been some interchange. Antonio is New Age. He likes to be told what to do by Higher Spirits, then 'he grows and he shares.'"

"You're being facetious? Aren't you always looking for teachers yourself?"

De Gier drank more juice.

"Good," the commissaris said. "Let me have your thoughts. What else does Grijpstra's report tell you?"

So far so good, de Gier argued, but Bert Termeer could, according to Bieber, be someone who had an unhealthy interest in little kids, a pedophile.

"Because the man sold pictures of Greek child wrestlers and homely bathroom scenes? Shouldn't we take note that Grijpstra checked for a record?"

Grijpstra had found no record but that didn't keep de Gier from defending his proposition. Old Termeer lived alone, and the connection with landlady and travel companion Carolien seemed like an early LAT—living apart together—relationship, so popular nowadays, preferred by couples who share abstract, but no carnal, interests. Jo Termeer had described Carolien as an attractive woman who liked to prance about in French underwear, was intelligent, a good travel companion, with a sense of humor. Bert Termeer still wasn't sharing his nights with her.

"Are you a pedophile?" the commissaris asked.

De Gier saw the point. Just living alone didn't necessarily indicate a sexual aberration. "But Bert Termeer did sell pedophilic literature, sir. And he did not live alone. There was the little live-in helpless nephew."

The commissaris nodded.

What Bert Termeer really liked was sexual play with little kids, de Gier proposed.

Not being checked by objections, de Gier now suggested uncle had abused nephew. He also suggested revenge, more than thirty years later. Jo Termeer falls into uncle's hands at age eight; nephew rips uncle to pieces after nephew turns forty.

"Raccoons did the ripping, Sergeant."

Yes, de Gier said, recalling the horrifying photograph of Termeer's remains.

"And then this murdering nephew bothers me?" the commissaris said. "And his former teacher Grijpstra? He alerts his own superiors, skilled criminal investigators?" The commissaris remembered sending his assistants to Crailo Golf Club. "Well, fairly skilled, in my case anyway...."

De Gier also remembered the golf expedition. He mentioned Baldert bothering the Crailo Rijkspolitie lieutenant, and later Grijpstra and himself. De Gier evoked an image of Baldert pathetically offering his wrists, begging for handcuffs.

The commissaris was rearranging his kiwi slices. "You see an analogy?"

Possibly. Both Baldert and young Termeer, de Gier now argued, were appalled at their own misdeeds, craved punishment, but had been too clever for their own good.

The commissaris nodded. So much for motive.

"The nephew has reasons to murder the uncle. You have thought about opportunity, have you?"

Was Jo Termeer in Central Park when his uncle died? Something for Grijpstra to check, de Gier said as he made a note on his napkin. He excused himself and walked over to the buffet to hunt for more juices. He selected apple and cranberry this time, carried back two tall glasses. He also found some yogurt.

The commissaris commiserated when de Gier could not eat the yogurt. "Poor fellow. What *did* you do last night, Rinus?"

De Gier looked pained. "What *didn't* I do last night?"

"With the police lady?"

"Not with the police lady, sir."

"But you were with her all night, weren't you?"

De Gier's mouth, in spite of all the healthy liquids he kept imbibing, stayed dry. He smacked his parched lips. "Yessir, I was. We tried, but then we didn't." He stared at his juice. "We fell asleep."

"And this morning?" the commissaris asked.

"She had left, sir."

"No note?"

"A pot of coffee."

"Stale?"

"Well yes," de Gier said, "she had to go work. I slept in."

"Dear me," the commissaris said.

The commissaris was glad, he told de Gier, that he had spent his virile years in a different, more fearless, period. "The years of breasts and penises," the commissaris whispered pleasurably, as he closed his eyes, enjoying numerous visions.

"You're feeling better, sir?" de Gier asked unhappily.

The commissaris apologized.

De Gier busied himself sipping alternate juices.

"U.S. immigration stamps all foreign passports," the commissaris said briskly. "Your suspect told me he had been here twice, once as a member of a guided tour group, once to investigate the alleged murder. If there are more stamps he will have to explain them. What makes you think that Jo was here in New York when old Termeer was killed?"

De Gier hesitated. Then he mentioned Road Warrior, a movie character. According to policewoman Maggie, a Road Warrior look-alike participated in the Central Park contest the Sunday Bert Termeer died.

"I'm not familiar with the character, Sergeant."

"He is an avenger, sir."

"Tell me the movie." The commissaris smiled.

"You're good at that. Remember the movies you told me when I was ill for a month? Every Tuesday and Thursday evenings. And when I saw them myself later they weren't anywhere near as good as you told them."

Chief O'Neill was on his way so there was no time for much detail. De Gier sketched the plot. Civilization, after a catastrophic global war, has come to an end. Homo sapiens is an endangered species. Somehow the Australian desert has escaped devastation in the atomic mayhem. Two small bands of desperados roam endless sand- and rockscapes in leftover automobiles.

One band is good. One band is bad.

In a conflict over the last supply of gasoline the good guys are losing to the bad guys.

Mel Gibson plays a lone warrior, detached, independent, driving a battered racing car, manned by himself and a feral dog, and revenging the atrocities committed by the bad guys on the good guys.

Jo Termeer had told de Gier that he liked "Australian futuristic bizarre action movies."

"But he didn't specify this particular Road Warrior movie, did he?"

De Gier made another note on his napkin.

"What are you writing, Sergeant?"

"Reminding myself to tell Grijpstra to investigate Termeer's interest in *The Road Warrior,* sir."

"Is this independent, detached Road Warrior character gay?" the commissaris asked.

Maggie had told de Gier about a previous Road Warrior movie entitled *Mad Max,* in which the same character appears as a heterosexual male whose wife and child are killed by bad gay guys. In the second episode of the saga, the one de Gier had seen, Road Warrior is too detached to show any interest in sex whatsoever. He does, however, get the eye from a woman dressed in white, but she dies.

"Bad gay guys figure in both movies, sir," de Gier said, "and Road Warrior manages to kill most of the fuckers. Sorry, sir."

The commissaris, tearing the skin of a mandarin, said "Aha, aha."

"It all fits," de Gier said triumphantly.

"If," the commissaris said, "Jo was in Central Park, and dressed up as this Road Warrior. This actor Mel Gibson is handsome?"

"Yes," de Gier said.

"Well, so is Jo Termeer. Black leather, I suppose? Boots? That sort of thing? Outfit all roughed up? Some dangerous-looking weaponry?"

"A riot gun."

The commissaris drank his coffee. "I could think of another more likely suspect, Sergeant. I think you could too."

De Gier, after many years of practicing the art of criminal detection, had no trouble changing leads. He dropped Jo Termeer without effort.

"Charlie," de Gier said brightly. "Termeer's neighbor. Charlie is often in Central Park. The man is very visible. I have three reliable informants who describe subject as an older muscular type of male, who drags a leg. He allegedly looks kind and prosperous. Subject is suntanned. He works out near the Natural History Museum. He is often accompanied by a seeing-eye dog, a large female Alsatian.

"One informant tells me Kali was also seen with Bert Termeer."

"Aha," the commissaris said. "Termeer didn't have bad vision, did he? Does Charlie have bad vision?"

"We'll know tonight, sir."

"Tell me about your informants."

De Gier specified:

1) *Antonio, a recovered alcoholic gay male nurse, an intelligent man living a disciplined life with a well-organized friend in a Horatio Street bed and breakfast, who visits Central Park regularly to sail his model boat. Antonio has often noticed Charlie. He also noticed the dog, Kali.*

"Aha," the commissaris said. "I like recovering alcoholics. Antonio knows the pair by name? There is friendship?"

"No, sir, I put in the names."

"Antonio saw Charlie in the park on the day old Termeer died?"

"He thinks he may have."

"Ah," the commissaris said. "Ah. The good Antonio

again. Didn't you say that Antonio knew Termeer too? Called him 'a prophet'?"

"Yessir, the two met. Termeer told Antonio 'to watch it.' There would be a philosophical implication."

"Please continue," the commissaris said. "Maybe have some coffee first? Let me pour it for you. Here you go. No sugar, a little milk. I'll stir it."

De Gier sipped gratefully, then continued.

2) *The Central Park Precinct's efficient and intelligent-looking uniformed desk-sergeant knows both Charlie and Kali by name. He didn't see them on the day Bert Termeer died.*

3) *Mounted Policewoman Maggie McLaughlin, a level-headed and intelligent person, knew both Charlie and Kali by name. She had told Charlie to keep the dog leashed, which he didn't. She was fairly sure she saw Charlie and Kali in the park on the day Termeer died.*

"Now it's the other way around," the commissaris said. "We have opportunity, but do we have motive?"

Chapter 18

The commissaris, in earlier, more positive and therefore more restricted times, used to say that "good luck comes to those who keep trying." He was lately heard to say that "good luck comes to those who are lucky."

Two events happened that afternoon. While the commissaris attended his lecture at One Police Plaza, where he viewed slides showing deadly weapons made from junk by handy criminals who, the burly captain lecturing said, "were out of cash but used these to get it," and while de Gier wandered about the magnificent display of Papuan art in the Metropolitan Museum, admiring wooden demons who sprouted other wooden demons out of the tops of their heads, Maggotmaid killer Trevor was shot dead in Central Park by Detective Tom Tierney.

Events that led up to Trevor's killing began when

Detective Jerry Curran, dressed as a hobo, overheard Trevor talking into a public telephone. Trevor, when repeating the other party's information, used the words "Zabar's" "NYNEX" and "Alice" and the code figure/letter combinations "1K," "2P" and "4P." Detective-Sergeant Hurrell cracked Trevor's code. He correctly surmised that Trevor was to meet his party at the bronze statue of Alice in Wonderland in Central Park at 2 P.M.

Both parties would be carrying shopping bags from the famous New York deli Zabar's. Each bag would contain a NYNEX phonebook. They would not greet each other but would sit down on the same bench. They would leave carrying each other's shopping bags.

If no police activity occurred, the parties would meet again at the Alice statue at 4 P.M. This time Trevor's bag would contain cash in the amount of the going wholesale price for one kilo of heroin and the other party's bag would contain the product.

When Hurrell and his two assistants attempted to arrest Trevor, who was carrying the heroin-filled shopping bag, Trevor pulled a pistol from under his jacket. Trevor's gun turned out to be unloaded.

Detective Tom Tierney's gun was loaded.

Sergeant Hurrell, later that same afternoon, walking contentedly through the park, noticed a derelict slumped on a bench. The man was wearing a dark brown tweed suit, complete with waistcoat, a quality shirt that had once been white, a plaid necktie, cream woolen stockings and leather boots that showed traces of polish.

The derelict, taken in by a patrol car summoned by Hurrell, admitted, at the Central Park Precinct, that he had robbed a body he'd stumbled upon. The man, drunk and stoned, couldn't remember when or where. "A while back." The derelict did say the body was dead "and bleeding."

Perhaps remembering that he had been on a higher level of existence once, he then rose laboriously, tried to strike an orator's pose and said "in theatrical tones," as Hurrell's report had it, that the body "had been urinating" and that he had found it "in the early morning hours."

Chief O'Neill, taking the commissaris home after the homemade firearms lecture, heard the news on his police radio. He stopped at the Central Park Precinct on the Eighty-fifth Street transverse and Hurrell showed him the confiscated clothes.

"No wallet?"

"No," Sergeant Hurrell said, "but check the trousers."

O'Neill noted that there were bloodstains around the fly area. The chief instantly created a theory. "So Bert Termeer had been peeing, had he? Poor fucker fell down, felt the need, opened his fly, peed, had his heart attack, thrashed about, flung his head this way and that, then— dentures flying every which way—he dies."

O'Neill wrinkled his nose in disgust. "Next thing, a raccoon locates his dinner. Tears off what Termeer had exposed. Hurrell's bum finds the corpse, strips it of its clothes, puts them on. Leaves his own clothes and his dirty blanket. The raccoon comes back, brings his family. The commotion attracts the park's carrion birds. Hawks peck the head, raccoons eat the lower torso.

"Right, Yan?"

"Why not, Hugh?" The commissaris looked at the blood on the tweed trousers that Sergeant Hurrell was holding up for his inspection. "Oh yes, Hugh, that could easily have happened."

Hugh patted Hurrell's shoulder. He smiled. "I think our case is definitely closed now. Nice work, Earl."

Chapter 19

The bellhop Ignacio, after he saw de Gier coming in to pick up the commissaris and observed the two men checking de Gier's map to find the location of Watts Street, Tribeca, insisted that they make use of the Cavendish's free limousine service.

The limo, exceedingly long and cumbersome even for that class of vehicle, got stuck in Canal Street traffic. The commissaris told the driver not to worry. He and de Gier could walk the short distance. After they got out traffic loosened up somewhat and the limo disappeared, taking with it de Gier's map, which the commissaris had left on the back seat.

"Watts Street," the commissaris said. "Should be easy. Lots of people about. They'll all know it."

De Gier, still focused on the Papuan ghost masks and soul boats that he had been looking at all afternoon, walked along dreamily.

Since they were now at Canal Street's eastern end, they would need, the commissaris explained, to walk all the way west, from the East River to the Hudson, and then, on Watts, they'd go south, aiming for the towers of the World Trade Center that no one could miss.

"Watts Street, Tribeca," the commissaris said, "short for *Triangle Below Canal.*"

"Okay," de Gier said.

"Charles Gilbert Perrin," the commissaris read from his notebook.

"Nice name," de Gier said.

"Charlie'll be there," the commissaris said. "At number two. I phoned. He sounded very pleasant."

"Good," de Gier said.

"You know," the commissaris said, "why, according to chief O'Neill, Hurrell didn't visit Charlie at home but just briefly interviewed him at the precinct? Because Tribeca is known for transvestite hookers. Because Hurrell's child died in Tribeca." The commissaris tsked.

De Gier tsked too.

Canal Street displays a seemingly endless array of market stalls on both sides. Food odors float on diesel fumes. Large buses and trucks thunder between overflowing sidewalks when they're not gridlocked between traffic lights. Policemen whistle at honking vehicles willing but unable to get going again.

"Watts Street?" the commissaris asked people of

different colors, each dressed differently from the others.

"Vots Strijet?" "Trots Strit?" "Zljotz Striet?" responded the different people.

A new flow of eager buyers pushed the commissaris and de Gier into a corner where they found themselves staring at a display of Chinese-made windup toys. Beetles, mounting other beetles, whirred furiously. Clowns tumbled. Flame-spitting monstrosities danced about. Rabbits tried to climb carton walls, fell back, wagged their tails, seemed to have digestive problems.

A little black girl with bright ornaments in her felted hair strings picked up toys that had stopped and passed them to a boy who turned the toys' keys and handed them back.

At the next stall a soup vendor tended a charcoal fire under large aluminum containers. Brown children dropped wilted vegetables, bloodied bones and fish heads into the containers' bubbling contents.

"Sopa?" the vendor asked, offering a bowl and spoon.

"No thank you, sir. Watts Street?"

De Gier listened to the voices holding forth all around him. The sergeant's linguistic interests were aroused. Hardly anybody spoke English. All these people might be recently arrived. Amsterdam is an international city too and de Gier had learned to distinguish sounds and phrasing to determine origins. He heard Chinese voices, both Cantonese and Mandarin, Arabic, Spanish. Tall women in robes might be Tibetan. Other tall women in robes might be Zulu. Two white shoppers coming by could be Finnish.

"Vot street you vont?" the soup vendor asked.

"Watts."

A woman directed them to a little folding table set up in a doorway where a beautifully bearded man in a turban and flowing robes sold light bulbs. There was the fragrance of quality marijuana mixing with that of incense burning under the oil-painted picture of a guru sitting in the lotus position.

"Watts Street?"

"What street?"

They left Canal, turning south at the next side street, followed an alley without a street sign, then kept turning until they saw the river.

"Maybe here?"

"I'll ask." De Gier strode over to a tall white prostitute in a miniskirt and a silk blouse under an imitation lynx fur coat. "Watts Street, please?"

"Right here." The prostitute's voice was a baritone. "All the way down to the Hudson River, but there's nothing here but warehouses and me. My minivan is around the corner. I work in the car. I could oblige you?"

"No thank you." De Gier looked for numbers. "Number two?"

"Bert and Charlie?" the prostitute asked.

The commissaris stepped closer, looking pleased. "Yes, do you know them?"

The prostitute looked suspicious. "You can't be cops, not with those accents."

"Cops from Holland," the commissaris said. "We're

just inquiring. Does Bert Termeer live near here?"

The prostitute shook a cigarette out of a Marlboro pack. "Got a match?"

"We stopped smoking," de Gier said.

The prostitute coughed painfully. "Good for you. I smoke because of the weather but the weather gets worse." He found his own match after digging about in a shiny handbag. He sucked smoke hungrily, coughed, sucked smoke again. "Termeer is dead."

"We know," the commissaris said. "That's why we're here." He put out his hand and said his name.

The prostitute laughed, then excused himself. "What sort of a name is that?" He shook the commissaris's hand. "My name is Teddy."

De Gier shook hands too.

Teddy walked them to a three-story warehouse with a crumbling cement-over-concrete front. Between rows of boarded-up windows apostolic faces, white skinned, black bearded, smiled appealingly. Birds held up banners. The banners bore a text:

give your time

do things for God

give your money

"Give your money to me," Teddy said. "I can use it. I badly need cough drops."

De Gier handed over a twenty-dollar bill.

Teddy thanked him. "Like to see my place on the Bowery? Best whips and chains collection downtown."

"Thank you," de Gier said. "We don't have the time." He pointed at the beseeching smilers, the text-carrying bluebirds.

"Termeer and Charlie put that up?"

Teddy laughed. "No, that was the Good Lord Club. The club didn't survive. The bank foreclosed and Charlie bought the building. There's nothing much here for Goodlorders." He waved at forbidding warehouses up and down Watts Street. "No conversions."

There were two sets of stone steps, each leading to a metal door. The commissaris tried to read a small hand-painted sign next to the left door. His outdated glasses failed him.

Teddy helped out. *Bert the Bookseller.*

"You knew Bert Termeer?" the commissaris asked Teddy.

Teddy grimaced. "Sure did."

"Did you like him?"

"I like Charlie," Teddy said. "Charlie asks me in when it rains. We eat noodles in the restaurant some-times." He raised a shoulder. "Just friends, you know? Separate checks. Regular conversation. 'Pass the soy sauce.' I like that. You know? Friendly-like?" He pointed at his pick-up spot on the corner of Watts Street. "The lamppost gets lonely. I take off for lunch. When Charlie wants to eat noodles and he happens to come by we go eat together."

"Termeer didn't ask you in when it rained?"

"Sure," Teddy said. "Oftentimes. Any kind of weather." He looked over his shoulder. A man was waiting at the end of the street. "Uh-oh. Duty calls, gents."

Teddy walked away, on long silken legs, swinging tight hips.

The commissaris and de Gier contemplated the door on the right side of the forbidding building. Charlie's nameplate was a strip of yellowing paper covered by cracked plastic. The writing was in black ballpoint.

charles gilbert perrin

The commissaris pressed an oxidized brass button. A loudspeaker spoke near his ear, uncannily clear of static, transmitting a calm deep voice.

"Nothing needed," Charlie said, "I thank you. Take care now. Okay."

The commissaris said his name.

"Mr. Dutch Police and Co.?" Charlie asked. "Stay right there, folks, I'm coming."

The commissaris looked down Watts Street, wondering how Grijpstra would like this view. Grijpstra might paint it on a Sunday morning, as a change from dead ducks. The commissaris thought that the narrow empty alley—not even cars were attracted to Watts Street— would inspire an artist searching for unusual settings. Watts Street's emptiness seemed intensified, perhaps because of the ghostly light reflected by the shimmering Hudson.

De Gier picked up on the atmosphere too. "An end-of-time street. Nobody here but the dead, sir. But they might be returning."

In the alley's massive gray and brown buildings nothing seemed to go on. Warehouses for stolen goods? Sweatshops where illegal aliens worked for low wages? The structures' formidable steel doors locked curiosity out.

Bolts were turning on the inside of number two.

The man who faced the detectives appeared to be a well-cared-for, friendly, healthy gentleman in his mid-fifties. The muscularity of Charlie's body, mentioned by Mounted Maggie and the desk-sergeant at the Central Park Precinct, hardly showed under a blue turtleneck sweater. Charlie's dark blond hair looked old-fashioned, cut short, shaved around the ears, slicked down, combed neatly. The face was naturally tanned and Charlie had recently shaved meticulously. Brown eyes sparkled behind metal framed spectacles. Charlie's large nose curved slightly. The teeth were strong and clean, with a single gold filling. Charlie's wristwatch might have been bought on Canal Street: a twenty-dollar digital item with a simple metal strap.

The commissaris handed over his card. De Gier said his name. Charlie read the commissaris's last name easily, without any accent.

Charlie smiled. "Step right up."

"You speak Dutch?" the commissaris asked, surprised at Charlie's faultless pronunciation of the many consonants in his long name.

"I lived in Aachen for a while," Charlie said, "just over the border. I sometimes went across and so I learned how to pronounce the sounds on your side."

"You speak many languages?" de Gier asked.

"Anyone," Charlie said, "who has to try to grow up the way I did better learn languages, my friend. Mine are, in chronological order, Yiddish, Polish, German, French and, last but not least, English. English"—Charlie smiled—"is easy to pick up, impossible to master." He beckoned his guests into a clean and empty red-brick hallway. "Always good to be fluent in communication when you're passing through hostile lands."

"Is Perrin a Polish name?" the commissaris asked.

"I was once called by another name, long ago, before World War II," Charlie said, "but there was too much blood on it. After I finally reached America I chose my own label. 'Charles' refers to my favorite author, Charles Willeford, a cheerful nihilist. 'Gilbert' is in homage to a schoolteacher I loved prematurely. 'Perrin' is a town in Maine I dream about when the wind goes the wrong way and Watts Street stinks. I sometimes go to Perrin to listen to loons."

"Loons sometimes chant with coyotes," the commissaris said. "Listening to the chant makes one replace wornout ideas."

Charlie laughed. "Exactly." He looked into the commissaris's eyes. "That's exactly right. You have obviously been there."

They followed Charlie, whose bad leg slowed him

down somewhat, into an old-fashioned industrial elevator. The cage-like cubicle was furnished like a room. The detectives sat on straight-back chairs while Charlie manipulated two long handles. On a card table a long-stemmed rose drooped gracefully from a slim vase. An Oriental carpet covered the floor.

"Why not?" Charlie asked. "Nobody likes cages. This lift has been everything. I like to go to auctions or find things in the street, use them, replace them. Last month this was a cabinet for albums of West African colonial stamps that I sold the other day." He waved. "A nonprofit hobby. I liked being able to live with those stamps, for a while. Wonderful colors. Nice little pictures. A chance to experience those colonial times. The lift also exhibited photos of Laurel and Hardy. I collected those for years, then gave them to a museum. Before that I tried to recreate a Maori temple with painted bamboo and a rattan floor. Before that, let me see...right, the complete works of René Daumal. Here, on that table." He faced his guests. "René Daumal? The name is familiar? No? It is not?"

The elevator stopped but Charlie didn't open the accordion door yet. "Daumal appeared as a French essayist and poet who wouldn't stay with us. Thirty-six years old in 1943." Charlie clicked his fingers. "Daumal's complete denial cheered me up completely. You really haven't read him?"

He looked at the commissaris. "*A Night of Serious Drinking,* or *La Grande Beuverie?* No?"

He looked at de Gier. *"Mount Analogue?* Unfinished. Because Daumal died halfway through the last, but not least, chapter. Of tuberculosis, like the parents of Willeford. Such a useful disease. Suddenly sets us up on our own. No?"

De Gier brought out his notebook and wrote down the poet's name and the titles.

"You're interested," Charlie said, sliding open the elevator's door soundlessly. Apparently it was well oiled.

The commissaris said that de Gier understood French and was always looking for nothing, "...and as you said that Daumal denies..."

Charlie concentrated on de Gier. "You know what I liked that Daumal said? No? Then I will tell you."

He help up a hand until he was sure he had de Gier's attention. "This is beautiful I think. *'Je vais,'* Daumal said, *'vers un avenir qui n'existe pas, laissant derrière moi à chaque instant un nouveau cadavre.'* Would you translate that?"

De Gier asked Charlie to repeat the phrase.

Charlie obliged.

"I go," de Gier translated, "toward a future that doesn't exist, leaving behind me, at every instant, a new corpse."

"Beautiful," Charlie said. He pointed at the elevator decorated as a Victoria boudoir. "I had all eight of Daumal's published books there. In various editions. I don't have them now. I only kept *Le Mont Analogue,* the one Daumal didn't finish."

The commissaris looked back at the elevator. "This is the way it's going to stay?"

"Is anything going to stay the way it is, ever?" Charlie asked.

"Your next project?"

"I have shelves holding up human skulls in mind," Charlie said. "I found some on Canal Street. Party stuff for Halloween, but good strong plastic. I knocked holes in them, tied them together and hung them in the river. I'll take them out in a month. Then I'll line them up on the shelves, out of order, some upside down, some on their sides. Make it look like Guatemala. Have a tape recorder play a Charlie Haden ballad whenever the elevator is activated." He peered into de Gier's face. "You like Charlie Haden?"

De Gier did.

"What does he play?"

"Charlie Haden plays double bass, sir."

Charlie held de Gier lovingly by the shoulders. "You're not applying for discipleship, are you? I don't teach, you know." He kept smiling and winking. "Just kidding, just kidding. Maybe I won't do the skulls at all, let them rot in the river." He looked cheerful. "What do you think of my other idea? A display of plywood dolls, flat like regular people, no depth to those dolls, have a piece of string dangling between their legs, yank the string and we're all waving and smiling."

The commissaris, still looking back at the elevator,

discovered a framed colored-in photograph of a red-haired woman with green eyes and milky skin hung from a metal bar.

"Carolien," Charlie said. "Bert's girlfriend. Now that Bert is dead I thought I would put that up, Bert's better side...."

The commissaris stepped back into the elevator to study the picture.

"It isn't really Carolien," Charlie said. "I found it in a junkyard the day I identified Bert's remains at the morgue. But she does look what Bert told me she looked like. I thought maybe he loved her."

Charlie led the way to his quarters through another empty hallway lined with scrubbed red bricks. "I live here, top story. Bert had the rest of the building. I may rent his part out, or donate it as a shelter."

"I heard," de Gier said, "you helped him with his mail orders. The book business. You don't plan to pursue that?"

Charlie shrugged. "Nah."

A dog was waiting in Charlie's open doorway.

"Hi, Kali," de Gier said.

The German shepherd, wagging her bushy tail slowly, offered the commissaris a paw and barked twice, solemnly and clearly. It greeted de Gier likewise. The dog pulled her paw back and walked ahead of the detectives, looking back to make sure they followed.

Charlie explained that his home used to be a factory loft, that he'd renovated. He had put in the hardwood floor himself, using remnants sold off by a nearby lumber-yard. The plastered walls were filled in some, then whitewashed. The solid mahogany roof beams were cleaned up with steel wool before varnishing, so that the gleaming old wood contrasted nicely with the heavy pine boards supported by the beams.

Several large easy chairs, a couch and a round dining table with unmatched chairs took their positions as museum objects representing disparate styles. A kitchen stove, two refrigerators and a washer and dryer, together with cupboards and open shelves, all dissimilar but sprayed the same off-white color, were lined up along the vast room's back wall. All furniture and appliances were clean and seemed to be in working order.

"Found it all," Charlie said. "All you need in Tribeca is a handcart and some free time. I found the handcart too."

The bedroom was an open garret at the end of the room, reachable via a metal circular staircase. An old-fashioned iron bathtub stood on a platform built out of heavy packing cases. A reading lamp was bent over the tub. A TV and VCR combination was set up to provide easy viewing for the bather.

"Entertainment corner," Charlie said.

The commissaris, accompanied by Kali, walked through the room—hall, rather. "You like empty walls?"

"Walls of the soul," Charlie said.

"Beg pardon?"

"Better to keep them empty."

The commissaris looked puzzled.

"But emptiness can be frightening," Charlie said. "The restless eye, you know. Always wants something to glance at." He looked at de Gier. "Do you read Sanskrit?"

De Gier did not.

"Neither do I," Charlie said. "Maybe I should cover the walls with Arabic script, that's quite artistic, all those scribbles and loops. Sanskrit is more odd, though."

The commissaris looked bewildered.

"Arabic," Charlie said. "Texts from the Koran. I know little about Islam, the less the better. Writing in unreadable hieroglyphs is Termeer's idea, by the way."

"Ah."

"Yes," Charlie said. "It wouldn't be difficult. I photocopy some good-looking Arabic texts up at Columbia University, or the Asia Society maybe, enlarge them, then imitate the writing by hand all over that empty wall." He waved widely. "Real big. I have the space there."

"That will inspire you?" de Gier asked.

"A faded purple shade on that broken white," Charlie said. "What was that? Inspire? Sure. I should think so."

"But Sanskrit texts would inspire you too?"

"As long as I can't read them," Charlie said. "Otherwise I would get caught up in surface meaning." He looked at the commissaris worriedly. "You know what I mean?"

The commissaris scratched Kali between her furry ears. She growled, not unkindly, them pushed him gently into one of the easy chairs. "And then you will whitewash those inspiring, but, to you, in the first instance anyway, incomprehensible, texts away again?"

Charlie watched his empty wall pensively. "Yes, after a while. Could be years, in fact, but I wouldn't keep them there forever. They would get old."

"You might even learn to read them." The commissaris laughed. "That's de Gier's problem too. How are you doing with your Spanish text, Rinus?"

De Gier had read his Alvaro Mutis novel in the subway that morning, without understanding much of what the writer was saying. Losing out on meaning he had been able to appreciate the poetry of Mutis's balanced and musical phrasing. "But when I looked at the pages again I did gain some meaning."

"Right." Charlie nodded. "I probably would too, looking at my Sanskrit texts from the bathtub. I'd get curious, go back to the library, do some studying. Reflecting." He shook his head sadly. "As I said, get caught up in their kind of, what's the word, *commonsensical* side?"

"Then what?" the commissaris asked.

De Gier looked too. "Paint it over. Books get lost. Walls get covered."

Charlie looked dreamily at his enormous blank wall.

"Would you leave the wall empty again?" the commissaris asked.

"I should," Charlie said, "but I think I'll draw future life forms." He took a sketchbook from a shelf. The pages were covered with drawings of beetles. Some insects were complete, others dissected with erect lower bodies—ready to copulate—long, gracefully bent antennae, multiple eyes, jaws with extending feelers, segments of wings.

"The future," Charlie said. "If I sit in the bath over there and watch the news then I know, like you know, like everybody knows, that we're coming to some endings."

"We humans," the commissaris said.

"We humans, sir. Can't handle our unlimited multiplication combined with destructive technology." Charlie shrugged. "No big deal." Charlie smiled. "There's always something else to follow."

Charlie predicted that a next evolution might be beetle-based. "Beetle-beings might do well for a while, until it all happens again: Intelligence improves, egotism remains, science doubles the life span so the population explodes, the beetle race self-destructs, like the human race before it."

"There could be changes," de Gier objected.

Charlie's theorizing changed direction. "What if it goes differently the next time?" he agreed. "What if beetle-beings get it together, learn to live in harmony? Does chaos tolerate contentments? Wouldn't another meteor hit the Beetle sapiens planet, wipe them out like the dinosaurs?"

"Ah," the commissaris said, not unhappily.

"You believe in an end to humanity, sir?"

The commissaris would not refuse to believe in lots

of little endings to lots of little things, like humanity, for instance.

"Soon?"

There were some signs, weren't there?

Charlie was surprised. "You're not an optimist, sir? So what do you bet on? We stupidly kill each other or a meteor does it for us?"

The commissaris thought either way would be just fine, but as Charlie said just now: There's always something else to follow. Personally, he was thinking more of jellyfishlike creatures as a form of future consciousness. Considering the given fact of ice caps melting, oceans growing, lands diminishing, one might predict evolved aquatic beings.

"Looking like jellyfish?"

"Mind if I get up?" the commissaris asked the dog.

Kali stepped back.

"Why," the commissaris asked as he walked about in Charlie's gigantic space, being careful with the tip of his cane so as not to scratch the hardwood flooring, "why would future life forms develop along lines easily imaginable by our kind of minds? We think of insectlike creatures because insects, like us, have faces, eyes, arms, legs. The future creature may not need any of those."

Charlie sat on the side of his bathtub. "No?" He nodded. "I see. Yes. Perhaps."

"Surely," the commissaris said. "The jellyfish, think of it. A semifluid transparent dome. It doesn't walk, it waves. It doesn't see, it feels with tentacles. Essentially different. It functions beautifully. Why should it be like us?"

"Mhree," Charlie said thoughtfully. "Yes. *Eerhm."*

"Pardon?"

"That's what Bert used to say," Charlie said. "That reality extends well beyond imagination. The weirder, the more real."

"The future could be something else entirely," the commissaris said. "Not only beyond our imagination, also beyond our memory. Our memory wouldn't be there, you see. It would have wafted away, along with ourselves."

Charlie wasn't listening. He bent toward the commissaris, arms stretched, palms up, as if to accept some worthy present. "And these jellyfishlike creatures? How would they go about perpetuating themselves?"

The commissaris was at the other side of Charlie's vast space and had to shout to bridge the distance. "Jellyfish can multiply like plants if they want," the commissaris shouted. "The creatures grow like fruits on a tree-like structure, but they also have sexual organs, which can be joined while swimming free. The future, like the present and past, will be exciting."

"Bert," Charlie shouted, "wanted you to go beyond all three of those stages."

"Bert had his penis ripped off," the commissaris shouted. "Do you know why?"

Chapter 20

Adjutant Grijpstra received de Gier's fax, transmitted after breakfast at the Cavendish, at 5:00 P.M., just as the adjutant was ready to go home to his empty apartment. He beeped Cardozo.

Cardozo, who, together with a fearful Turkish/Dutch interpreter, was listening to a taped shouting match between leaders of rival protection rackets operating in Amsterdam's Old West section, the new Turkish quarter—a cacophony of exotic swearing that provided no information—was glad to come over.

"More bullshit from our roving Sergeant Bogus," Grijpstra said. "What do you make of this?" He read de Gier's faxed questions: Where was Jo Termeer on June fourth? What is Jo Termeer's interest in *The Road Warrior* movie?

Cardozo didn't feel like trying to interview Jo

Termeer again, not even with Grijpstra's hairy hands dangling above his curls. He suggested seeing the movie. "Might give us ideas. We can see Jo later."

Cardozo was ordered to go rent the movie. He bicycled about and checked with three different video-rental stores. *The Road Warrior* happened not to be in stock. He bicycled back to headquarters, quiet now but for Grijpstra's drumming.

"Right," Grijpstra said, putting his sticks down. "If Jo Termeer has some special interest in the movie he is likely to own it. Go find him, go find the movie. Call me. We will all watch it together."

Jo Termeer could not be found, either at his place of work, the hair-care salon in the fashionable suburb of Outfield, or at his luxury apartment, above the hair-care salon.

"Who did you talk to?" Grijpstra asked.

"To his partner," Cardozo said. "A certain Peter."

Grijpstra crushed the paper cup he had just filled with coffee from the machine in the corridor outside his office. He hadn't drunk the coffee yet. He walked about his office watching his steaming thighs.

Cardozo brought a towel.

"You're smiling," Grijpstra said. "Don't smile. Peter? That would be Termeer's lover, yes? Where is the printout of the original complaint? The hullabaloo that got all this started."

Cardozo and Grijpstra read the report together.

"'Nature person,'" Grijpstra said. "That's what Termeer called Peter. 'Nature person Peter.' Black guy. De Gier liked him. Let's go see Peter, Simon."

It was the era during which Amsterdam was beginning to tackle its traffic problem. In order to discourage vehicles from using the congested quaysides, parking-meter rates had been tripled. Offending cars were towed quickly or immobilized with steel clamps, removable upon payment of a large fine in cash. Police vehicles, unless marked as such, were no longer exempt; detectives were beginning to use public transport.

It was raining and the bus was first late, then slow. Grijpstra hummed a song at the bus stop and napped while the bus heaved its way through traffic.

"Food first," Grijpstra said, seeing an elegant bistro next to the hair salon "Jo and Peter."

Cardozo looked nervous.

Grijpstra let Cardozo pick their table. The adjutant remembered Cardozo liked lentil soup, veal croquettes on French bread, applesauce on the side, a Hero brand fruit drink with the meal, a double espresso afterwards. Grijpstra ordered all the items. He complimented Cardozo on his recently dry-cleaned corduroy suit and his haircut of that morning.

"Looking good, Simon, looking good."

Grijpstra grabbed the check. He paid. He tipped.

"You're all right?" Cardozo asked.

"I'm teaching you something." Grijpstra laid a

protective hand on Cardozo's shoulder. "You figure out what."

Cardozo knew what. "Not to rely on…"

"Shsshshsh, my dear Simon."

Grijpstra and Cardozo strolled into the hair salon and confronted Peter.

Peter, who met de Gier's description of being "a slender, active, intelligent forty-year-old black male, fashionably dressed," was busy. He had two clients in chairs, more waiting. Peter came over, scissors in one hand, comb in the other. "Can I help you, gentlemen?"

Grijpstra showed his ID. "We would like to see Jo Termeer." Cardozo said hello.

"My partner?" Peter looked at Cardozo. "You were on the phone just now, yes? I told you already. Jo isn't here." He pointed at the waiting clients. "He should be. What can I do?"

"Sick leave?" Grijpstra asked.

Peter sighed. "More like personal leave, I would say."

"Problems?" Grijpstra asked.

Peter nodded. "It's your investigation, I think. About that American uncle. The delay is driving Jo crazy. He wants to know what's going on but he knows he should be patient. I've told him to do his police job, the reserve thing, but I think he prefers cruising." Peter laughed. "Being naughty."

Clients clamored loudly.

"Anything else I can do for you?" Peter asked,

glancing over his shoulder. "I'm coming, dears."

"The Road Warrior," Cardozo said. "Would you have that movie? We would like to see it."

The request didn't seem to surprise Peter. He gave them his keys to the upstairs apartment that he and Jo shared and told them to help themselves. Videos were on the shelf, alphabetically arranged. Coffee and cookies were in the kitchen. The remote was on the TV. "I'll be up in about an hour."

The detectives watched the movie in the apartment's living room, furnished mostly with glass and leather. A large painting above the fake fireplace showed slim cowboys in tight jeans and leather vests leaning across a counter. The videotape was worn out in parts. Halfway through the movie a young man let himself into the apartment. "Hello?"

Grijpstra put the VCR on pause. "Hello. Who are you?"

"Eugene," the long-haired semi-Oriental-looking young man said. He showed Grijpstra his perfect profile as he turned towards Cardozo. "And who, may I ask, the fuck are you two?"

The detectives got up and showed their IDs.

"Peter let us in," Cardozo said. "He'll be up in a minute. You live here too?"

Eugene lived elsewhere but he was a friend of the family, "so to speak." He waved at the TV. "Couldn't you find something else to watch? Every time I come here Jo has *The Road Warrior* going. I know every scene backwards."

Grijpstra pressed the remote's power button. "You don't like Australian futuristic bizarre action films?" He muted the sound of roaring engines as Mel Gibson, by suddenly accelerating his racing car, tricked the skinheads on their powerful motorcycles. The bad guys attacking the lone avenger from either side now shot little arrows into each other. Or so it seemed. Wide wavy bands cut through the images and made events hard to follow.

"It's okay," Eugene said, pouring himself coffee, "but after a dozen times or so you kind of know how Good conquers Evil and after two dozen times or so you sort of start wondering what's so good about Good."

"Jo's favorite movie, right?" Cardozo asked.

Eugene sighed. "Isn't it ever."

The movie had ended when Peter came in. Eugene and Peter embraced tenderly, then kissed.

"Busy day," Peter said, still hugging his friend. "How did you like Jo's alter ego? Do you know Jo had made himself a Road Warrior outfit? And that he has a car just like that thing in the movie? A hot-rod horror?"

Grijpstra and Cardozo got up, thanking Peter for his hospitality. "It was nothing," Peter said. "You're welcome. Anything else perhaps?"

Now that Peter mentioned it, Grijpstra said, there were just two more things. Could Peter tell him where Jo was on June the fourth and could he perhaps show them

Jo Termeer's passport?

"Really…," Eugene said. "What are you guys after? Isn't a passport personal? Is this The Return of the Gestapo? Why…"

Cardozo moved forward. "We can come back with a warrant. Now if—"

Peter stepped between the belligerent parties. His voice was soothing. His gestures were mild. "Now, now…now, now…sit down, my dears. Listen. Hear the thrush singing in the park?"

Everyone listened. A thrush, indeed, was singing.

"Adjutant," Peter asked, "would you care to pour more coffee? A slice of cake, anyone? Baked this myself. Won't take no for an answer." He presented the tray. "Okay? Can I get the passport from between Jo's clean shirts without you two starting another war here? I can? That's nice."

Jo Termeer's passport showed two sets of entry and departure stamps applied at Kennedy Airport. One entry dated two years back. The other was recent. June 7 through 10.

"So," Grijpstra said, "Peter, tell me, was Jo here June fourth? Working with you downstairs in the salon, living here in the apartment?"

"Sure," Peter said.

"Did you see those perverts kiss?" Cardozo asked when he and Grijpstra were waiting at the bus stop.

"Aren't Jo and Peter supposed to be a couple?" He snorted. "I would call that adultery, those guys are no good."

"Well now," Grijpstra said, "adultery, adultery...I'm afraid that idea is extinct now, Simon."

Cardozo disagreed vehemently. He referred to acceptable social mores, to behavioral limits, to love being related to trust, to there being such a thing as decency "even in sick relationships, I'll have you know."

The bus arrived. Grijpstra pushed Cardozo ahead of him. "You're a dear boy," Grijpstra said after they were seated. "Old-fashioned, behind the times, limited, I'm not saying 'retarded,' mind you, restricted perhaps, well meaning in a kind of useless way...."

Chapter 21

The commissaris, that evening, unable to sleep after the long-legged tram-driving demon once again tried to get him to do something he didn't understand, and that, he felt sure, he wouldn't want to do if he did understand, used his ivory bedside phone to wake Katrien.

Katrien, blinking at early sunlight pouring into the bedroom's windows on Queens Avenue, Amsterdam, said she would make coffee and return the call, once she was washed up somewhat and settled on the veranda.

It took her twenty minutes. The commissaris had dozed off. The Number Two streetcar was pushing through traffic, clanging its bells which became the telephone on the night table, ringing.

It took him a while to accept the change from streetcar to phone.

Katrien was unhappy. "Jan, what kept you?"

"I couldn't pick up a streetcar, dear."

"Your dream again? You feel better now?"

He did now that he heard his wife's mothering voice. He sketched, briefly, succinctly, the reasoning that had made him and de Gier decide there was another suspect and how he had devised and applied a trick to try and shock Charles Gilbert Perrin into opening up.

"A ripped-off penis," Katrien said. "Isn't that the worst that can happen to those who have one? Doesn't that make ripping it off a heinous crime? How did the suspect take your sudden outburst?" She watched a row of tulips that hadn't been pushed over by Turtle yet. "Tell me everything, Jan."

Charlie, the commissaris reported, had taken the outburst calmly. But there had been a change of atmosphere that he set about to repair.

He guided—his bad leg dragging more noticeably—his guests to the dining table, where, with the dedication of a priest serving mass, he served iced tea and seaweed biscuits.

Kali sat on a chair too, lapping water from her bowl after gently pushing the glazed biscuits away with her nose. Charlie said that he regretted what had happened to his tenant, acquaintance, friend if you like.

He had known Bert Termeer for some years. Nobody likes to lose a friend. But, Charlie said, what happened had to happen.

How so?

Because Bert Termeer thought of himself as bad.

How so?

Because Bert Termeer knew that Bert Termeer was sneaky.

Charlie said that "externalization is the beginning of liberation." He also said, "We have to be open about what we are. That is, if we want to solve the problem."

"The personal problem?"

Why not? But Charlie also, more particularly, meant the overall problem. He had been attracted to Termeer by the man's sincere quest for—Charlie smiled at Kali, who had pricked up her ears, as if she were going to hear something worthwhile—Termeer's quest for what? For seeing through the human condition? "All that activity in book trading, in playing the fool—'God's fool,' that kind of role is called in religion...."

They had come to the end of the iced tea ceremony by then and were being taken on a tour of the building.

Charlie unlocked and pushed and pulled huge doors, walked the detectives through hollow-sounding corridors that led to Termeer's part of the building, in and out of another elevator (a bare cage this time), even made them climb a ladder to inspect the building's attic.

Charlie led the way, Kali guarded the expedition's rear end.

Kali even wanted to climb the ladder. The ladder was deemed too steep by Charlie but Kali nudged de Gier, got him to pick her up, turn his back to the ladder and climb its rungs with his heels.

De Gier cradled the dog, who kept perfectly still, resting her long snout on his shoulder. The attic was filled with piles of unsorted books and pamphlets.

The commissaris inspected Bert Termeer's private quarters, bare as a monk's cell, uncomfortable but for the huge water bed. Termeer's printing shop contained outmoded equipment, used to manufacture his monthly catalogue. Empty cartons and rolls of packing paper were stacked.

Then there were, in the basement, props for Termeer's former acts.

"You think that was worth the trouble?" the commissaris asked, picking up and putting down a trumpet, holding up a monkey-size robe and hat.

"Producing, directing, acting out a show that might liberate people from dead-end routines?" Charlie became enthusiastic. "Sure." He nodded. "That's why I let Termeer live here. I thought we might have fun together. Test some theories. Do some philosophizing. Get weightless together. There was a time I thought I might join in his performance."

The commissaris was grinning. Charlie grinned back. "You would like to do that yourself, wouldn't you? An adult version of throwing water balloons at folks?

"And," Charlie said, "Bert wasn't a do-gooder, like the outfit that I bought this building from. The give-time-give-money-do-things-for-God crowd. Not that," Charlie said, pulling a face. "No. Never."

"You don't care for do-gooding?" de Gier asked.

"Please," Charlie said. "After my Polish Experience?" He shrugged. "Yes, sure, maybe for a little while. Set the needy up till they can take care of themselves again. I wouldn't help anyone to prolong his misery, though. Encourage depression?" He made a fist and pounded his palm. "Set them free, let them go. Don't shackle them with welfare."

"You set up Bert Termeer here?" the commissaris asked.

Charlie held his head to one side. "Yes. Sure. When I met Bert in Central Park, years ago, we had this conversation. I had some apples. I asked him if he wanted one. He said he would take the apple if I would give it to him without using my hands. I told him he could have the apple if he took it without using his hands."

"Zen," de Gier said.

Charlie nodded. "We had both read the same book on Zen koans."

"Same level of insight," the commissaris said.

"Right. But it didn't mean much. Exchanging book knowledge doesn't, you know. I thought we had a beginning. Bert wanted to get into New York, he was living in some flophouse, and I had all this space here—I got the building cheap from the do-things-for-God-folks—and Bert might have explored avenues I hadn't even thought of yet so I loaned him money and charged minimal rent."

"Did he pay you back?" the commissaris asked.

"Some," Charlie said. "Yes. Little by little."

"And Bert impressed you?"

"Look at this," Charlie said, sweeping his hand toward a long row of figures lined up against the room's wall, representing a single person's (Bert Termeer's own) physical lifetime changes. "That plate on the left—can you see it?—holds a microscopic object, a fertilized human egg. The plate on the right—can you see it?—shows remnants of a human bone."

Dust to dust.

"Of course," Charlie said, "'dust to dust' is still something.

"One should really look left of the embryo, where there is nothing, and right of the bone crumbs, where there is nothing again."

"Nothing to nothing."

And, Charlie said, what Termeer had wanted to show Sunday morning crowds in the public parks of Boston, Massachusetts, and Bangor, Maine (the Central Park authorities had thrown the exhibit out), after he had put up his line of figures, a tiring exercise since some of them were heavy, was that there was nothing in between the two nothings either.

Termeer's show—nothing, to rapidly changing embryos, to baby, to toddler, to little kid, to kid, to young adult, to grown person, to middle-aged man, to codger in increasingly debilitated and demented stages, to corpse, to skeleton, to crumbling bone, to nothing—highlighted a common denominator: lack of substance.

No substance to the body. No substance to the mind.

"Would you," Charlie asked the commissaris, "accept as your essence your aches and pains?

"Would you," Charlie asked de Gier, "accept as your essence your guilts and depressions?

"So what are we?" Charlie laughed. "I liked Termeer's implied line of questioning. It was in all of his shows. Even here in New York. A dignified gentleman ruminating in an exaggerated pose. A dignified gentleman frolicking in childlike joy."

They all looked at all the Bert Termeer's again, standing at the far side of the room, with porcelain faces, each showing the aging process, the right clothes, thickening, then thinning hair, giving way to baldness, all different shapes, only sharing a name.

The commissaris said that. "They're all Bert Termeer."

"My name," Charlie said, "was once Paulie Potock. Would you say I am that frightened little boy in Poland? Would you say I am the frightened old man who is told by the doctor he has Alzheimer's disease?"

"You think you might have that?"

Charlie waved indifferently. "Brain tumor, colon cancer, whatever we die of these days, irreparable blocked arteries…"

"But," the commissaris asked, "your friend. Bert

Termeer. Wasn't he just another faker?"

Charlie patted Kali's head. "No. Not altogether. I think Bert did have true insights. Eh?" he asked the dog. "You liked Bert, didn't you? When you were with him in the park? You would bounce about and play?"

"A prophet?" the commissaris asked.

"Oh yes."

"What didn't you show us?" the commissaris asked, after twisting his painful hips so that he could face his suspect.

"What didn't he show you?" Katrien asked on the phone.

"But he did show me," the commissaris said, "in that very building's dank dungeons."

What Charlie showed the detectives in the badly lit basement was Bert Termeer's second activity, another mail-order business, also complete with all it needed: an antique press, an obsolete but functional labeling machine, shelving, boxes, packing paper, rolls of packing tape, stocks of product.

The piles of imported magazines Charlie kicked around in the basement—while Kali crouched, growled, even howled with fury—the imported videotapes Charlie roughly pushed off their shelving, the posters and pictures he picked up and tore in half mostly showed small children being tortured.

Chapter 22

De Gier, agreeing with the commissaris that the job was done, spent the night at Horatio Street after losing at playing darts with Antonio and Freddie. He also telephoned Maggie, apologized for making a mess of a potentially beautiful experience and invited her to dinner the next day at the Italian restaurant. She said she didn't think so but to phone her in the morning. He slept well, phoned Maggie again, was told by her answering machine that if it was he it was okay, walked to Bleecker Street and took the subway. The commissaris invited him to breakfast at Le Chat Complet, where no cats walked past the high windows and where nobody sang.

Grijpstra's report on Termeer's alibi, faxed to the Cavendish and brought along for de Gier to read—the commissaris had trouble with the fax's faint lettering—

confirmed that Jo Termeer was no longer a suspect.

De Gier said that he knew Charlie was involved when Charlie, the suspect, asked de Gier, the investigating officer, to translate Daumal's poetry, which said, "I go toward a future that doesn't exist, leaving behind me, at every instant, a corpse."

"A corpse, sir." De Gier cut his French toast. "Why bring up a *corpse*, for Christ sake, and *he* left it behind, and *at every instant*, like he couldn't get rid of it, like he kept dragging Termeer's body with him?"

The commissaris nodded although he could think of quite a different interpretation. The quotation could refer to another level. The poet Daumal could have referred to man's continuous change, leaving behind him used thoughts, used actions. The commissaris was going to tell de Gier that when Mamère came by to pour more coffee.

"You dream better now?" Mamère asked. She rushed off before he could answer. The commissaris sighed. He dreamed worse. The tram driver had been back that night like every night, and the hellish presence was more persistent than ever. Although he felt better physically—the coughing and sneezing attacks had stopped, even his hipbones smouldered less—he dreaded falling asleep, knowing the tram driver would be waiting, talking infantile gibberish while she showed her long legs and pursed her luscious lips. The gibberish was more high-pitched now. The phantom was getting impatient, the sacrifice she needed was long overdue.

The commissaris had to attend one more lecture, and he invited de Gier to accompany him to One Police Plaza. The subject was child molestation. The lecturer was a medical doctor as well as a clinical psychologist. The black Philadelphia-based expert started off with simple cases featuring bruises and broken bones. She progressed to the more nebulous area of strange stories accompanying urinary tract infections and bed-wetting. She spoke about the inability of the victims to testify. She mentioned the customary reluctance of family and concerned parties to cooperate.

"Most of what is out there," the doctor said, "we'll never know about, unless we learn to pay attention."

After the lecture de Gier went off to spend the afternoon with his Papuan statues at the Metropolitan and to see Maggie afterward, and Chief O'Neill and Detective-Sergeant Hurrell took the commissaris out to lunch at a Korean restaurant on Columbus Avenue in the upper nineties.

O'Neill had closed the Bert Termeer case, "if there ever was one." He did regret the way the corpse had been ripped up by raccoons. O'Neill had heard that the Urban Park Rangers meant to start hunting raccoons. He raised his glass. "To the Rangers."

Central Park, Hurrell said, was known for its begging squirrels. Squirrels had learned to sit up for peanuts, and some had even mastered the art of shaking hands.

And Central Park was also known for its rats. Rats

looked like squirrels; their lack of plumed tails was not noticeable when they faced little old ladies. Rats liked peanuts too, he said. Rats had learned to join squirrels when little old ladies handed out peanuts.

Rats didn't shake hands, though. Rats bit.

So many little old ladies had been bitten by rats that another admonition was to be added to the park's notice board:

DON'T SHAKE HANDS WITH RATS

The commissaris raised his glass again at the end of Hurrell's topical story.

The commissaris was taken back to the Cavendish. He thanked his hosts for their hospitality and assistance.

"Any time, Yan," O'Neill said.

"Glad to be of help," Hurrell said.

Lying back in his hot bath, the commissaris reconsidered his and de Gier's recent reasoning.

There was sufficient psychological motive to justify accusing Charlie of murder. Termeer's shadow side had disgusted Charlie. Charlie had learned that his tenant didn't just operate the catalogue business but actively participated in perversions.

After he showed them the basement, Charlie had told the detectives that Teddy had complained about Termeer's insistence on sadistic/masochistic acts that, even for good money, were too painful. "The man is a meanie," Teddy said.

Teddy had also seen boys enter by Termeer's separate

entrance and had tried to warn them off, but the boys had to finance their habits. Charlie finally learned why Kali whined and growled when Termeer was entertaining company in his part of the building.

Charlie told the detectives that, after having listened to Teddy, he had checked Termeer's premises, using his duplicate keys.

"We heard that you sometimes helped Termeer with his holy book mail-order business," the commissaris said. "But you say you had no idea of what was going on in the basement?"

Charlie said that he hadn't spent much time with Termeer in the last few years, that his fantasy of working with a kindred spirit had come to an end long ago. Termeer, although maybe able to perceive further than most, had turned out to be dour, twisted into himself, hardly civil most of the time, moody, even boring.

"You were unaware of Termeer's dark side?"

Charlie had no idea until he lunched with Teddy at New Noodletown in the Bowery.

"Recently?"

"Yes."

"How long before Termeer died?"

Charlie calculated. "A week? Ten days?"

"You confronted your tenant?"

Charlie had been considering a confrontation, but then there was no need.

"Where were you when Termeer died?"

Charlie said that he might have been in the park, or else on his way home. The park had been too busy that day.

"Did you see Termeer in the park that Sunday morning?"

"Yes."

"Did you talk to him?"

"No."

"Why did you inquire about Termeer at the Central Park Precinct the next day?"

Because, Charlie said, Kali had been restless all night, pacing and whining. Charlie himself also had a bad feeling. He had let himself into Termeer's part of the building early the next morning. There was no one there, which was unusual because Termeer enjoyed his water bed and liked to sleep late.

"Why," asked de Gier, "did you tell us Termeer's death had to happen?"

Charlie sighed. "Because he couldn't allow his personality to corrupt itself further."

"He didn't kill himself, did he?"

"No."

"He was killed?"

"Yes."

"Did you kill him?"

"No." Charlie smiled. "No, I didn't. I wouldn't kill anyone. I will not defend the world by using violence. I prefer escaping."

"Really?" the commissaris asked. "You don't say.

What if you couldn't escape any further? You would jump, would you?"

Charlie smiled. "But of course."

"And you wouldn't take anyone with you? A few bad guys? To feel better?"

"Nah," Charlie said. He shrugged. "Fuck the bad guys."

De Gier was still pursuing his original line of reasoning. "Why didn't you kill Bert Termeer? There was your immense disappointment in a man you had sponsored, there was fury, there was opportunity, you're a very intelligent man, Mr. Perrin, you could have come up with some excellent plan, you..."

Charlie said he had been thinking of calling the cops, of showing them Termeer's basement.

"What if the cops took no action?"

But they would have, Charlie said.

Charlie's fatal attack on his tenant, the commissaris thought in the Cavendish bathtub, would have been planned carefully.

Charlie knew Termeer would be freezing and frolicking in the park that Sunday morning. Charlie would know about Termeer's bad heart. A performing Termeer would be vulnerable. All Charlie had to do was hover about, wait for the crowd to focus its attention elsewhere, grab Termeer, drag him into the bushes, yell accusations in his face, shake Termeer violently, terrify him until he suffered a heart attack.

There were the dentures, found at some distance from Termeer's corpse. The dentures flew out of Termeer's mouth as he was crying, begging for forgiveness....

Good luck comes to those who are lucky, the commissaris thought, letting more hot water into his tub by twisting the faucet with an extended toe. There was Maggie's big chestnut horse kicking Termeer as an unexpected preliminary.

Now came the theory's weak part.

The commissaris agreed with de Gier that Charlie could be excused for wanting to punish a child pornographer posing as a prophet. Shaking and slapping? Okay. Castrating a former friend?

And again, the commissaris thought, good luck comes to those who are lucky. The corpse was robbed by a derelict, then partly eaten by animals.

No witnesses, wounds, clothes, prints, traces.

"Let it go, sir," de Gier had said during the return trip on the subway. "We have no jurisdiction. The local police are hung up on another theory. All the evidence is long gone. Our suspect is intelligent, unwilling to confess, sympathetic. The victim was mad and bad."

"And dead anyway."

The commissaris couldn't see himself bothering Paulie Potock, one of the few Jewish children to survive the Nazi atrocities in Poland. After the basement revelation, back in Charlie's artistically pleasing environment, the commissaris had inquired into Charlie's painful past and the source of his present comforts.

Charlie talked easily, breaking out the cookies again. "Japanese," Charlie said. "Advanced food. There is a nice store in SoHo. Seaweed is the future."

"How did you get out of Poland, sir?"

The detectives saw Paulie, together with forty-eight other Jewish Polish little kids, guarded by two SS men, march, with a few surviving mothers, to Nowogrodziec Railway Station.

March 1945: The Russian Third Army was close. The Nazis were emptying out all death camps. A train waited. Boxcars closed off with barbed wire were to take the Jews to Germany to be killed, but Soviet war planes dived and set the train on fire.

It had been snowing heavily. The children and the mothers marched in singe file. Paulie was trying not to drag his bad leg. The mother up front sang out: "One, two, *three*."

In order to obey the guards but to delay reaching the platform, where, because of the train not taking them to Germany, all prisoners would surely be shot, the column moved forward on "one" and "two" but stepped back on "three."

The SS men, older soldiers, tired too, stumbled along.

The German forces had long since run out of motor fuel.

The SS men disappeared into the woods when they

heard a rumble of powerful engines.

The column stopped when black spots appeared on the eastern snow-covered plain.

The spots were little tanks that grew in size as they came nearer.

The huge tanks stopped close to the standing column. From the tank turrets jumped older kids, Russian tank soldiers.

The Jewish Polish kids were in the eight-to-nine-year-old age group and the Russian soldier kids were in the fourteen-to-fifteen-year-old age group.

March 1945: The Russian army had lost ten million young and middle-aged male and female soldiers. Old folks manufactured deadly equipment to be handled by kids.

Once liberated, Paulie, without relatives but knowing by now how to take care of himself, lived here and there, and finally moved to America. He worked in a bank. He received money from the new Germany government, *Wiedergutmachungs* Funding, "money to make good," a fairly large amount that he invested profitably. He also went crazy. He was institutionalized for depression. A Chinese-American psychiatric nurse suggested the patient should write a list of things he liked, and brought him a new pencil and a sheet of white paper, which Paulie destroyed.

Every day the nurse brought fresh paper and another new pencil, which Paulie tore up and broke, until, one pleasant morning, there was a sparrow on his windowsill. Charlie watched the sparrow, then wrote his list of Nice Things to Do. Watching seals off the Maine Coast would be nice. Having a dog would be nice. Starting his own growth fund would be nice. Owning lots of private space would be nice. Arranging temporarily owned objects would be nice. Laying an assorted hardwood floor— changing his name—working out in Central Park—would be nice. It would be nice to speculate as to what would happen (Charlie had read some Nietzsche by then, and tried to follow existentialism) to his state of mind if he removed the concept of selfishness from cynicism.

The commissaris wanted to leave but de Gier, who had been guided to and from the bathroom by Kali, asked how Charlie had found a seeing-eye dog.

It was the other way around, Charlie said.

The dog had approached him when he was working out in Central Park. The dog was scooting along on her bottom, trying to get the path's gravel to scratch her infected and blocked anal glands.

The dog was an Alsatian; in the death camps the SS had used Alsatians to terrorize the inmates.

Charlie walked away but the dog ran after him, sat on the path and offered her paw.

Charlie took the dog to an animal clinic. A vet squeezed the almost bursting glands empty and prescribed medication. Charlie bought a bag of food and emptied it out in the street. The dog ate everything and barked her thanks.

On the way home Kali—he had named her by then—didn't allow Charlie to cross a street against a red light. She pushed his leg when the end of a sidewalk came close, or when roller skaters got near.

Charlie visited the Lighthouse, the society for the blind, which promised to make inquiries about a lost seeing-eye dog. He was called a week later. A woman, who wouldn't give her name, said her blind husband had died and that she had abandoned his dog in Central Park. "You keep her. I never liked her."

The woman hung up.

Chapter 23

The commissaris, dozing off in his bathtub, faced the long-legged tram driver. De Gier, musing in the Metropolitan Museum, faced a Papuan demon sculpture.

Both detectives, at about the same time, felt a wave of serious and multiple misgivings. The wave wiped out their conclusion that Charles G. Perrin could be controlled by evil. He could not. Therefore he could not commit evil either. Charlie castrate Bert? Never.

The commissaris, wide awake now, clambered out of his bathtub, dried himself and dressed quickly.

De Gier left the Metropolitan Museum and walked to the nearby Cavendish.

The commissaris planned to face the hollow-eyed tram driver directly, to pull the phantom out of her hazy dreamscapes.

The commissaris and de Gier met in the Cavendish's lobby, where they were greeted by Ignacio. *"A sus ordenes, señores."*

The detectives found comfortable armchairs.

"Charlie is a good guy," de Gier said. "Don't you think so, sir? That dog, the way he treated that dog, and even better, the way the dog treated Charlie. I should have seen that."

"Yes," the commissaris said.

"Also the general atmosphere of Charlie's part of number two Watts Street," de Gier said. "I felt happy there."

The commissaris had felt happy too.

"And," de Gier said, "there was the tea ceremony, and all that hoo-ha about the elevator—that was nice, didn't you think so? Moving about in an exhibition that moves? And the empty wall with the invisible incomprehensible Sanskrit...."

"Arabic," the commissaris said.

"Arabic," de Gier said, "and the way he had fitted that hardwood floor together, that was beautiful. I thought, you can look at those patterns when you feel bad and it will be better. And that one, two forward in Poland and three backward...."

The commissaris agreed.

"So he didn't do it," de Gier said.

The commissaris thought that might be a possibility, but he wanted to know why the hollow-eyed angel wouldn't leave him in peace, and now he meant to see the voodoo lady.

Ignacio was asked to telephone Mamère. He came back to say that Mamère was home and expected to see the commissaris within the hour.

"A hundred bucks," Ignacio said. "Bad dreams don't come cheap."

De Gier checked his map. Ignacio helped him locate Brooklyn, Flatbush and Nostrand Avenue beyond Flatbush and told him where to catch the Number Five train.

The detectives sat quietly in the subway.

The Nostrand Avenue block where Mamère lived consisted of three-story buildings, with stores on the ground level, some separated by small alleys.

Mamère's was one of the better buildings.

De Gier waited in a coffee shop while the commissaris rang the buzzer and then hobbled up the steps.

Mamère, after pulling the blinds of her small sitting room and diffusing the light to please the spirits, sat in a large yellow reclining armchair and the commissaris sat in a large orange reclining armchair. Mamère's dog, which she told him was the grandson of the dog in the painting at Le Chat Complet, lolled a long red tongue out of its furry black face.

"*Les dol-lars?*" Mamère asked.

He handed them over: two twenties, one ten, one fifty.

"*Merci.* You relax now, don't care about nothing."

Nothing would please the commissaris more. He semi-dozed while Mamère hummed, then sang a fairly long song. African West Coast, the commissaris thought, although he hadn't been there. Toward the end of the song the commissaris lost his mind, although his mind never left the room, for he saw it float around Mamère's potted plants and the budgie birds in their multistoried bamboo cage, waft through the eyes of an alligator skull on a sideboard, then whirl about in the smoke of smouldering herb leaves.

He really liked being mindless.

Mindless, he saw Road Warrior drag a white-bearded man into some bushes. It didn't matter that the commissaris hadn't seen the movie and that he had never met Bert Termeer. There they were, Road Warrior screaming abuse, Bert Termeer whining for mercy.

Road Warrior shook the old man like a dog shakes a squirrel. Termeer lost his dentures. The commissaris saw Road Warrior bend over the helpless body of his enemy, saw a sharp blade flash and blood spout. He saw Road Warrior emerge from flowering azalea bushes, a zombie from the grave, moving one foot, the other foot, one foot, the other foot.

He didn't see the hollow-eyed long-legged beautiful blond angel. He asked Mamère about the angel when she let him out. "Someone you know?" Mamère asked. "More *dol-lars* sometime soon?"

"The angel drives a tram, Mamère."

"You can't trust angels," Mamère said.

"I saw Road Warrior and he wasn't Charlie," the commissaris said, "as I knew all along, and didn't want to know all along. I was sorry for the fellow, and I was flattered, of course. Coming to me, the Grand Old Man of Crime Detection. What did I see coming? What did you see coming? Did you see the uncle-loving nephew, fellow cop, fearless street fighter, Grijpstra's star student?" He glared at de Gier. "The truth, Rinus, stares me in the face, and my mind rushes off to look for lies. How many times has this happened?"

He sat next to de Gier in the coffee shop, sipping weak coffee and eating a donut as if that is what you do after having lost your mind for a while, then, alas, regained it. You sit in a coffee shop, between big black men on small stools, and you ask for more weak coffee and another donut.

"You know what you get when you eat a donut?" a man wearing a baseball cap the wrong way around told another. "You get a zero with the ring removed."

While riding the Number Five train back to Manhattan, de Gier wrote to the commissaris's dictation. De Gier got off at Fourteenth Street to make his dinner engagement with Maggie and the commissaris got off at Eighty-sixth Street to fax his notes home.

Chapter 24

"Now what?" Grijpstra asked, reading the commissaris's latest fax. "How many fourths of June do we have here, eh?"

He put the paper down, staring at it furiously, then brightening up. "Cardozo!"

Cardozo grunted.

Grijpstra's smile widened. "Let me tell you how you do this. You really disliked that Eugene character, didn't you?" Grijpstra beamed at Cardozo, slumped behind de Gier's desk. Grijpstra suddenly scowled again. "You *did* dislike him." Grijpstra thumped the desk. "AM I RIGHT?"

Cardozo opened long-lashed eyes. "I dislike all assholes."

Grijpstra nodded. "Good, good, good. Tell you what you do. You go and find this asshole Eugene, and you meet him somewhere...lemmesee, lemmesee, what's a good place for two assholes to meet...?" Grijpstra looked out of the window, into the cruel yellow eyes of a sea gull flying by. "How about Vondel Park?"

Cardozo stared. "Meet to do what?"

"You extract information."

Cardozo grunted.

"Information as to Jo Termeer's whereabouts on June Fourth this year."

Cardozo straightened up. "We've already done that, remember. You asked Peter?"

"Phone Peter now," Grijpstra said. "Peter will know where to locate Eugene. Phone Eugene and tell him you want to meet him in Vondel Park. Today. At sunset."

"You want ME to tell YOU about my good friend Jo Termeer?" Eugene asked. "A STORM TROOPER interviews a FAIRY? Are you going to BEAT me?"

Cardozo and Eugene strolled along Vondel Park's main path. Evening fell.

Cardozo fell too, because Eugene had hooked his foot behind Cardozo's leg and put his hand against Cardozo's chest. Eugene's leg pulled, Eugene's hand pushed.

Cardozo fell, head over heels. Cardozo stood.

Eugene and Cardozo laughed. They were two karate students exercising in Amterdam's most beautiful park, between ponds where exotic ducks floated about slowly, giant carp patroled leisurely and cranes stood on one leg under ornamental shade trees.

Eugene, being the winner, shook hands with Cardozo, who was the loser.

Eugene's hand squeezed painfully. Cardozo's thumb pressed the back of Eugene's hand. Cardozo moved his other hand under Eugene's elbow. Cardozo pushed Eugene's elbow up and Eugene's hand down.

Eugene yelled and sobbed.

"Swan-wrist hold," Cardozo said. "I could have broken your arm. You want that? You don't want that." Cardozo smiled. "Now tell me everything about Jo Termeer."

Cardozo fell again, because Eugene had hooked his foot behind Cardozo's leg again and put his hand again Cardozo's chest again. Leg pulled, hand pushed.

This time the falling Cardozo pulled Eugene's arm while he kicked Eugene's knee. Cardozo jumped up again, Eugene groveled in the gravel.

"Baboon's knee," Cardozo said.

"Don't you two lads have anything better to do?" asked an elderly lady. She helped Eugene up. "You two go and study Rudolf Steiner."

"Yes, ma'am," Cardozo and Eugene said.

"But for now you can help me feed the carp."

The elderly lady, Eugene and Cardozo fed a long stale baguette of French bread, which the lady broke into small pieces, to the giant fish of Southern Pond. Greedy ducks standing on racing carp approached at speed. The ducks held out their wings to keep their balance. As the carp stopped to feed, some ducks kept going and crashed into the pond's raised shore. Other ducks fell sideways, tumbling, like long-lost friends meeting, into each other's wings. Other ducks managed to hold on, making their steeds flap muscular fish tails to free themselves.

"You two behave now," the elderly lady said. "I can't be everywhere to save you poor fellows."

Eugene and Simon sat on a bench and rolled cigarettes.

"Tell me all about Jo Termeer," Cardozo said.

"Say 'please'?" Eugene asked.

Cardozo offered a light. "Say 'thank you.'"

Cardozo's report, delivered to the commissaris as soon as he and de Gier got off their KLM Boeing, stated that, about a year ago, Eugene had linked up with Jo Termeer and Peter in a Long Leyden Transverse Street gay bar.

The three pals wined and dined together and shared holidays abroad. Peter liked to go steady. Jo liked to cruise. Peter had an even temper. Jo was highly strung.

Jo, Eugene stated, had become impossible to be with after his interview with the commissaris. He didn't show up at the hair salon much and neglected his duties at Warmoes Street Precinct. He hung about the apartment. Then, when he heard that the commissaris had gone to New York, Jo began to drink heavily and to stay out nights.

As to where Jo was on June 4, the day of Bert Termeer's death: Eugene was told Jo was walking about the Ardennes Mountains region alone. Neither he nor Peter had heard from Jo for a few days, there were no calls or postcards and Jo had brought back no mementos from his foreign journey.

Interesting fact: Jo, while on holiday on the French Riviera, about a year ago, with Peter and Eugene, had said he'd lost his passport and obtained a new one at the Dutch Consulate in Marseilles.

When asked why he was so forthcoming Eugene stated that he and Peter had changed their minds, that they now thought that solving Jo's problem would be a good thing for all parties concerned.

Chapter 25

Two days after the commis-
saris's return, Jo Termeer was arrested after having been
thrown out of the Warmoes Street Precinct, Amsterdam,
three times within three hours.

Jo worked out of the Warmoes Street Precinct when
he did duty as a reserve constable-first-class. The sergeant
was disappointed to see Jo, whom he knew as a reliable
and capable colleague, turn up drunk and disorderly.

Jo, dressed in a torn-up black leather suit and muddy
boots, wearing a tattered leather gun belt and carrying a
wooden copy of a riot gun in a strangely shaped holster,
kept bothering the sergeant.

The first time Jo came in, the sergeant tried to treat
the matter as a joke. His colleague must have been playing
charades at a party. "Great act, Jo, you go home now." Jo
laughed and left. When, a few minutes later, Jo staggered

into the precinct, the sergeant had him removed by force. The third time Jo stumbled into the precinct he was arrested on a drunk charge and locked up.

When Jo's cell door was unlocked the next morning he wouldn't leave. The desk-sergeant remembered that Jo had been a pupil of Adjutant Grijpstra.

Jo wouldn't talk to Grijpstra at first but Grijpstra managed to cajole/threaten him into his Fiat Panda and took him home to Outfield where Peter cleaned him up.

The commissaris telephoned Peter that afternoon and asked him to bring Jo and Eugene to his house on Queens Avenue at nine that evening.

Cane chairs had been arranged on the veranda. Five chairs formed a crescent, opposite two chairs that faced each other.

Katrien put coffee on and cut up cake before leaving the house to visit with the neighbors.

The commissaris had the center seat, between Grijpstra and de Gier. Cardozo and Eugene sat on the end chairs.

Jo Termeer, wearing the same neat clothes as when he confronted the commissaris previously, sat facing Peter.

In spite of the formal setting everyone seemed relaxed, even jolly. The sky was clear, a breeze cooled the garden after a fairly hot day. Willow trees intertwined their branches on the street side. Their foliage screened the garden from cars swooshing by and the clatter of electric streetcars that liked ringing their bells.

"Is this a trial?" Jo asked before sitting down.

The commissaris said it could be, if Jo would like that.

"Are you the prosecutor, Peter?" Jo asked.

Peter said he would play any part that was required.

Jo told Grijpstra that he would prefer to be tried in a courtroom, with real judges in robes and lawyers and armed guards. Grijpstra explained that that would be difficult to arrange "for lack of reasonable cause."

"You know that, don't you, Jo?" the commissaris asked. "I've checked your file. You passed your criminal law examination with honors." The commissaris smiled his appreciation. "Now *you* tell me what the police could come up with to sustain a charge that earlier this month *you* killed your Uncle Bert in Central Park in New York."

Jo, elbows on knees, chin on hands, spoke to the floorboards of the commissaris's veranda. "Surely someone saw me dragging Uncle Bert into those azalea bushes?" He looked up anxiously. "You did check with that sergeant?"

"Hurrell?" the commissaris said. "Yes, I did. Sergeant Earl Hurrell says no one saw you near the scene of the crime."

Jo thought again. "The mounted cop, the beauty with the ponytail on the chestnut horse. *She* saw me."

"Not near the azalea bushes," de Gier said. "Police-woman McLaughlin saw a Road Warrior look-alike near a bandstand, too far away to be identifiable. I interviewed the policewoman several times."

Jo nodded. "I bet you did, Sergeant."

"Yes." De Gier looked away from smiling faces. He scratched his thigh. "Sure."

"Listen," Jo told Peter. "Let's start at the beginning. I was in New York at that time. You know I have two passports. My new passport was stamped. That's proof, isn't it?"

"I believe you destroyed your new passport," Peter said. "I believe it was a replacement for the one you said you lost on the Riviera."

Jo's muscular hands patted his knees. "Yes." He addressed the commissaris. "Maybe Kennedy Immigration has a record of my arrival. I made four trips in all, sir, three to shadow Uncle Bert, to find out what his routine was, and the fourth to kill him. Every time I arrived at Kennedy my passport was stamped. They have computers there; don't they retain such information?"

"I don't think so," the commissaris said.

Cardozo spoke up. "I checked with the U.S. Embassy. It's the same routine at Kennedy Airport as here at Schiphol. If everything looks okay no notes are made."

Cardozo and Eugene served coffee and cookies.

Turtle emerged from the long weeds bordering the commissaris's unkempt lawn. The company watched the reptile, on his way to a dish of lettuce, plod steadily along.

"I heard about your turtle," Jo told the commissaris. "Nice pet."

The commissaris smiled. "He is a friend, Jo."

Peter waited until Eugene and Cardozo had returned from the kitchen to ask Jo whether he had murdered his uncle.

"Sure," Jo said. "I planned it and I did it. Things worked out fine. The horse kicking Uncle made his heart play up. All I had to do was aggravate that condition."

"There is no proof you did any of that, Jo," Grijpstra said.

"How can you say that, Adjutant?" Jo's deep voice reverberated under the veranda's low roof. "You should have seen the mess we made. We were rolling around on the ground. I slapped his face. I put my knee in his balls. I shook him until his dentures went flying. I tore my nail when I was holding on to lapels of his jacket. I banged his face with the top of my head."

De Gier shook his head. "No traces, Jo."

"Please," Jo said. "What about all this DNA testing you read about in reports? What about boot prints? I have just read an article in *Police Weekly* that says a boot print is all a detective needs now." He held up a finger. "One boot print, Sergeant! I must have left hundreds."

"Jo," the commissaris said. "Sergeant Hurrell showed you Uncle Bert's body. Animals ate a good deal of it. The clothes found with the body were left by a robber. The robber and the animals erased your prints."

"Did you castrate your uncle?" Peter asked.

Jo was watching Turtle chomping a lettuce leaf.

"Tell us whether or not you cut Uncle Bert," Peter said. "I think you want to tell us that."

Perhaps the breeze changed direction, opening up the willow leaves, or it could be that a passing streetcar had an unusually loud bell. The tram's clanging penetrated the garden.

Jo was babbling now, talking about liquidating filthy perverts, which should be okay. There were all these perverts around abusing little boys. Jo kept repeating himself, mentioning his parents, who might have had problems, lovers, debts, what the hell, but they weren't gay at least. His dad and mom were just fine, they had him, didn't they? A little son, people like that, having little sons, to carry on their name, inherit the farm, and then Uncle came, and he was nice, yes goddamn it, Uncle Bert was nice, he, Jo, would never say he wasn't. They had gone on boats on the Amstel River together, and they had played at home, Sunday mornings, with a zoo that Aunt Carolien gave him for his birthday, and she unwrapped the plaster-of-Paris animals from the special silk paper that kept them from getting hurt, and he and Uncle Bert put all the animals between their little wooden fences, or in iron cages, and that's where they belonged, and sometimes Uncle Bert got the model train and made it go on rails looping all under and around the dining table, those were great games, and for lunch Aunt Carolien would make little pancakes, with ginger jam, but then after she left, Uncle would do those goddamn things damn it...."

"Jo," Peter said quietly, "Jo? Can you hear me? Look at me, it's me, Peter. Eugene is here too."

"I am here," Eugene said. "We're all here, Jo."

The garden on Queens Avenue was quiet again, until, from the next house, softly, punctuated by the hollow tones of a wooden drum, came the sound of a sutra being chanted in Sanskrit.

How frightening, the commissaris thought. Am I the only one who knows that this is about the void, that there is neither wisdom nor any attainment, that there is nothing to attain, that there are no obstructions and therefore no fear, that there is no ignorance, and no ending of ignorance, no suffering, no cause of suffering, no cessation of suffering, and no path, and here we pretend to sit around being busy?

"Did you cut him?" Peter asked. "Are you sorry that you cut off his penis, is that what has been bothering you? Do you want us to forgive you?"

Jo was being Road Warrior now, driving his supercar across the Australian desert looking for perverts who had ended his hope of having a wife and a child, like the good people in the farmland north of Amsterdam, where his dad and mom had him and where it had all been just fine for a while.

"Just a little counseling," Eugene whispered to Grijpstra. "That's all he needed. I told him that, but he was always so uptight. But maybe he didn't ever have a chance. Once they are raised in strict dualism—Dutch

Reformed Country Church—and then, suddenly, there is the permissive city here, add abuse to that, call up guilt, provoke lying and twisting to get out of that guilt…"

Jo looked at the commissaris. "Uncle was alive when I cut him." Jo got up and looked down at the commissaris from his great height. "I wanted you to find out, and now I want you to tell me about it. What do you make of this, sir?"

Peter stood next to Jo. He had his arm around Jo's shoulders. He asked Jo what the commissaris could tell him. Since when is a policeman a judge? Jo should thank the commissaris, who had done all he could, had investigated a crime, had located the guilty party, but couldn't dispense justice.

Jo howled, then cried.

Eugene got up. "Well, you know," Eugene said, "you have to figure this out yourself, Jobo. You did it, but you did it stupidly, because you wanted to be caught by the little old father figure, or rather"—Eugene looked at the commissaris—"the little old grandfather figure." Eugene punched Jo Termeer in the stomach. "Your stupidity is your cleverness. You left some psychological traces but this is the physical world, Jobo, the Justice Department is into sperm and blood." Eugene rubbed Jo's cheek affectionately. "Look here, if you want approval of your homemade morality, applause for Road Warriors of the Mind who castrate and kill uncles…eh." Eugene patted Jo's other cheek. "Tell you what, let me get you into a place in the country, nice and quiet, where you can figure things out and Peter and I will come see you."

"You're not a psychologist, are you?" Cardozo asked Eugene.

"He is," Peter said. "Eugene works for the Top Job Institute; he helps pick the chief executive officers of the future."

Jo sat down. He was calm now, momentarily in control of his emotions, de Gier thought. He had seen that happen before—murder suspects, during intense interrogation, unexpectedly becoming lucid.

"If I did the right thing," Jo said pleasantly, "I was ahead of my time. Present-day morality does not excuse the castration of abusive and perverted uncles. Commissaris?"

"Jo?" the commissaris asked.

"You can't get me a trial? Nothing you can do, except this"—Jo gestured—"meeting with sympathetic authorities, unofficially, while I'm in the company of my pals?"

"I'm afraid not, Jo."

"But by being bad I created my demon," Jo said. "I can't stand my demon, sir. She is driving me crazy."

"The Bad Conscience Demon," Eugene told Cardozo when it was all over and de Gier was pouring cold jenever from a stone jug and Katrien was handing out peanuts and the commissaris was talking to Peter and Grijpstra to de Gier and Turtle was sleeping between his favorite rocks. "Did you ever study Hieronymus Bosch's paintings?" Eugene asked Cardozo. "They crawl with Bad Conscience Demons. It would be interesting for you to do that, you being a copper. We live within a certain morality, the rules of our time, and then we break those rules, and thereby create our demons. They're totally unreal but we feel we have to appease them anyway." Eugene looked gloomy. "Or suffer forever after."

That was hours after a streetcar rang its bell at the tram stop behind the willow trees, and Jo jumped up and thanked everybody for everything and said he had to go now.

Chapter 26

The accident that killed Jo Termeer was reported by the crew of a patrol car called by the tram driver via her radio.

The policemen's report said that, according to the tram's passengers, the victim came running toward it well after the streetcar, of the Number Two line, had pulled away from the Queens Avenue tram stop.

A modern streetcar's safety features do not allow the vehicle to drive off when its sliding doors are still open. No system, however, is foolproof. This time the vehicle's safety feature didn't work. The streetcar's doors were still closing as the vehicle gathered speed.

The victim managed to jump through the closing doors but slipped on something inside the car—what that could have been hadn't been determined. It could have been anything—someone's spittle maybe, fruit juice, a crushed sweet. The passenger then fell over backward and, as the doors were still closing, his body was pinned between them. His head was still outside the tram and it hit the concrete base of a light post that marked the end of the tram stop.

The Number Two streetcar's driver, tall blond twenty-nine-year-old Agatha Franken, an experienced operator with an unblemished record, had not been aware

of anyth

stopped

Franken

where s

Th

after a

good a

and to

M

ing at

wife, l

back t

H

been r

Head